2⁹⁹

MW00596734

I,

DRAGON

MY NAME IS
SIMON

BY
NATHAN RODEN

I, DRAGON
MY NAME IS SIMON

Copyright © 2016 by Nathan Roden

All rights reserved. No part of this book may be reproduced in any form or by any electronic or mechanical means, including information storage and retrieval systems, without written permission from the author, except in the case of a reviewer, who may quote brief passages embodied in critical articles or in a review.

This is a work of fiction. Names, characters, places, and incidents either are the product of the author's imagination or are used fictitiously, and any resemblance to actual persons, living or dead, events, or locales is entirely coincidental.

www.nathanroden.com

GET **SIMON'S VOYAGE**
THE PREQUEL NOVELETTE
FOR FREE AT
WWW.NATHANRODEN.COM

GET BOTH OF THESE STORIES FROM THE WORLD OF WYLIE WESTERHOUSE FOR FREE AT WWW.NATHANRODEN.COM

ONE

Simon's sixth name day was the greatest day of his life.

Prince Simon Morgenwraithe fidgeted as he waited in the hall outside of the throne room. The new robe that had been made for the day's ceremony made his skin itch.

It was customary in the Kingdom of Morgenwraithe that the heir to the throne was announced before the people on his seventh name day. But King Bailin took particular joy in creating his *own* traditions. And in his mind, his son was so gifted beyond his years that there was no need to wait.

"Be still, young prince!" his mother's handmaid whispered into Simon's ear. "You will soon wave from the balcony to the people who will bend their knees before you. If you spend the entire time *scratching* that is all they will remember."

"If I had known the robe was going to itch so badly I would have washed it myself," Simon said.

"There was no time," the handmaid said. "The King gave us little warning he planned to make your announcement *today*. It is so exciting!"

The handmaid squeezed Simon's shoulders.

"We are so proud of you!"

Simon smiled, but his happiness was incomplete. He wished that these words came from his mother. But it had been so long since his mother had shown him any affection he could hardly remember it.

Simon looked around the room.

"Where is Lucien? Will he not be coming to watch?"

Three-year-old Lucien was Simon's only sibling. Yet, Simon hardly saw Lucien at all.

Lucien cried almost constantly, and spent most of his days attended by nursemaids. Simon had never seen the King hold the baby. The King and Queen spent virtually no time with their youngest son.

Simon had heard the stories, whispered among the castle servants.

The Queen was feeding the infant Lucien one day when the King's beautiful young seer walked past her. The girl smiled shyly at the Queen. The Queen flew into a rage.

The story whispered among the nursemaids was that the Queen had thrown baby Lucien across the floor. She never nursed the baby again.

Simon watched his mother as she crossed the room. He studied her eyes, as he always did, hoping to see something other than madness and hate. But that was all that he saw.

He watched her slip away from the frantic servants. She walked to a far wall and stood next to a dark and mysterious lady. They exchanged whispers, and then the Queen walked into the throne room.

Simon stared at the dark lady. She did not look at him. The woman was tall and thin. Her shiny black hair flowed into a lacy black dress that trailed the floor. Simon had never seen her dressed any other way. She had very long fingers, with long nails. And there was *something* about the woman that Simon did not like. She had never spoken directly to him. She smiled at him in passing, which always made his skin crawl.

Simon had seen his mother with the dark lady several times of late. This disturbed him greatly.

The dark lady's name was Magdalena. Simon did not believe she deserved such a beautiful name. He thought it more fitting that she be called "spider" or "witch".

Simon heard his father before he saw him. King Bailin had the perfect voice for a King. From his balcony, he could speak to thousands without even shouting.

Simon's heart leaped when he saw his father.

When he saw his father's *brother*, his heart sank.

Simon had been determined to gain his father's love and affection for as long as he could remember. It fueled his every desire: his desire to walk, to talk, to master language, to master reading and writing, and to learn the history of the Kingdom. His earliest memories were of his desperate desire to gain his father's attention.

And his efforts had worked.

But the King's brother, Lord Sterling, also coveted the King's attention. Sterling always had a cup of wine or ale in his hand, and he was forever putting a cup into the hand of his brother.

And so, on Simon's sixth name day, Bailin and Sterling were reeling from the last night's drink.

Simon rubbed his sleeves briskly one more time. He stood straight and tall.

King Bailin walked toward the balcony. He waved and addressed the people. He turned and held out his hand for the Queen to join him—

And then hell itself descended upon Morgenwraithe Castle.

A dagger flashed—a young girl's throat exploded in an eruption of blood. People ran in every direction, screaming. The servants that had surrounded Simon were gone. He tried to see what was happening. He heard his father bellow in agony. His father came toward him—

But then the King's eyes grew wide and blood gushed from his chest.

Simon looked into the far corner where the dark lady had stood. She was still there.

And staring directly at him.

The dark lady held her fingers in the air and pointed at him. Her hair swirled around her head, crackling with light, without the aid of any wind. Her eyes flashed with the same madness as the Queen's. Her lips moved, but Simon could not make out any words.

The itching became intolerable. Simon tore off his robe. He opened his mouth to scream, but the sound that escaped was like nothing he had ever heard.

The rush of screaming people halted. The screams died down. The crowd of people in front of Simon backed toward the walls, leaving Simon the view of a lone woman on her knees in the middle of the room.

His mother.

She was covered in blood from her hair to her feet. She clenched a dagger in her right hand. Her eyes blazed with ultimate madness. She pointed at him.

"Behold! Your new King!" she screamed—
Before she plunged the dagger into her heart.

Simon had no time to react. The screaming began again, and men ran at him. The King's Guards charged him with hate-filled eyes and raised swords. Others reached to pull arrows from their quivers.

Simon turned to the side to seek his escape. He lifted his arm—

Only, it was *not* an arm.

It was a...a...

Simon saw the glint of steel as a sword swung down at his side.

He almost collapsed. His right side exploded in pain.

Simon turned and ran toward the balcony. He looked down.

His feet, were no longer *his* feet. He hovered above the floor.

This is not possible, he thought. *This is all a dream. A nightmare!*

Arrows flew past him.

Simon reached the balcony and threw himself off of it. The death from a fall had no face—and no name. The same brave men who had sworn on their lives to protect him were now chasing him with hatred in their eyes, and foul words on their lips.

Simon squeezed his eyes shut as he fell. His instinct to survive overtook him and his arms beat against the air.

He slowed. And then, he rose into the air.

Simon opened his eyes.

He had no arms.

He had *wings*.

A flurry of arrows bounced off of his scaly body. The wing cut by the sword had grown numb and stopped bleeding. Members of the King's Guard mounted horses and screamed with hate-filled voices as they chased after him.

Simon turned toward the west, and the setting
sun.

He flew, and he cried.

TWO

Twelve Years Later

The dragon woke to the sound of barking hounds. He had flown many miles from the cave that was his current home. He dared not do what he was about to do anywhere near his secret lair.

The dragon hid behind trees at the edge of the forest. His scales faded to match the mottled gray of the tree bark.

He watched silently as the hunting party passed by and then continued to the north. The dragon crept along, keeping the dogs in sight. They sniffed at the ground and the air as they ran ahead of the men.

The dragon spotted the prey before the dogs did. When the hunters caught sight of the solitary bull elk, they quickened their pace. The dragon stepped out of the trees behind them and took flight in the opposite direction. He flew low over the trees and circled back toward the elk. He heard the thrum of arrows, followed by the baying of the hounds and yells of men.

"I got him! The kill is mine!"

"You're off your head, Crager! You'll find my quill in the neck of that bull!"

The dragon tucked his wings and dove.

"Look there! The dragon!"

"Now there's the kill I've been waiting for! Out of my way!"

"There is the hide that will feed me for the rest of my days!"

Arrows flew past the dragon. A dozen of them bounced off of his scales. He swooped low and latched onto the massive bull elk.

"Ooof!" the dragon strained at the elk's weight.

"I'm sorry," Simon whispered to the dead animal.

He flapped his wings with all his might until the curses and screams of men and dogs faded into the silence of empty sky.

THREE

The dragon soared along the treetops with the setting sun at its back. The man was ignorant of the dragon's presence. He concentrated on unhitching his horse from his plow. In the blink of an eye, the dragon swooped and wrapped his talons beneath the man's arms.

Four children screamed and ran to their father. Two young girls in long dresses huddled together as two older boys screamed curses and threw stones at the great flying beast. The dragon and its catch were out of sight within seconds.

"No!" the man screamed. "My children! Let me go, foul creature! My children—they are all I have!"

Seconds later, the dragon descended to the mouth of a cave. He released the man gently to the ground.

"Are you hurt?" the dragon asked.

"Y-you...you speak?" the man shuddered.

"Ha, ha, ha!" the dragon chuckled. "I am a gifted foul creature!"

The man spat on the ground and lifted his chin.

"What else but a foul creature would take a man

from his family just to fill his belly? Well, get on with it! Roast me with your demon breath!"

He threw his arms out to his sides.

The dragon shook its head.

"Where is the children's mother?"

The man dropped his arms.

"What? You have no right to—do you mean to fill even my last moments with torment?"

"Where is their mother?" the dragon asked softly.

"She…died," the man said. "She took the fever— three winters past."

"I counted four children."

The man balled his fists.

"If you touch a hair on their heads, I will haunt you from the grave! I swear it!"

The dragon raised a leg and pointed a talon at the man. The man flinched and turned his head aside.

"I need your clothes," the dragon said.

The man blinked hard several times.

"What?"

"I said I need your clothes. Quickly, please."

"I do not underst—"

The dragon drew himself to his full height and spread his wings. His eyes changed from dull amber to a blaze of orange fire.

"I do not HAVE ALL DAY!" the dragon's voice shook the earth.

The man sat on the ground. He took off his boots and his socks. He stood and shucked his trousers and shirt.

The dragon raised his talon again. The man closed his eyes.

"Please…"

The man waited for death. When it did not come, he opened one eye.

A filthy old blanket hung from the tip of the dragon's talon.

"Take it," the dragon said. "You will suffer many thorns on your journey home."

The man took the blanket and put it around his shoulders. He looked around.

"Where are we?"

The dragon pointed.

"Walk due west. You will find an old path that will take you downhill to the river. Follow the river upstream. Your farm is not far."

The man stared at the dragon for a few seconds. He nodded and took a few steps west. He turned.

"I don't suppose I could keep the boots? Or my short sword?"

The dragon shook his head.

"No. Sorry."

The man nodded. He took a few more steps and turned again.

"Any chance I could get my clothes back—when you're done with them? I don't have many."

The dragon raised his head into the air and breathed deeply. Four feet of flames shot from his nostrils.

"Never mind! Never mind! I'm going!"

"Stop!" the dragon said. "I did not mean to threaten you. The fire—it often comes without my intent."

He hung his head.

"When I am done with the clothes, they won't be worth having."

The man walked away.

"Could I ask a favor?" the dragon asked.

"You ask a favor?" the man said. "From me? Are you serious?"

"Please, speak of this to no one," the dragon said.

The man shook his head and turned to leave for the final time.

"Who would believe me?"

The dragon watched the man disappear into the trees.

He spoke to himself.

"When I take my rightful place on the throne, then all people will believe you.

"And King Simon will never forget you."

FOUR

Simon stepped outside of his cave just before sunset. He watched the last of the day's sun disappear. He focused on his breathing and tried to stay calm.

And he waited.

The intense pain was something he never grew accustomed to. As the full moon breached the horizon, his transformation began.

His wings drew inward. They shrank in from the tips with an awful cracking sound. The wings receded into his back and shoulder blades in a process that consumed two full minutes.

Simon tried to contain his cries, but he failed—as he always did. His anguish grew from a whimper to a scream and finally erupted into a blast of fire that reached forty feet into the night sky. With the full moon in place, Simon completed the transition from a two thousand pound dragon—

Into a one hundred and ninety pound man.

"There it is! There's the fire! Sound the horns!" the

shouting came from the river, on the downstream side. Simon heard the voices and the blare of the horns in the darkness.

He trembled on the floor of the cave. His skin burned hot. His back and shoulders screamed out in pain as he pulled himself to his feet.

He would not have much time.

Simon hurried to pull on the clothes. The socks were threadbare and both of the boots had holes on the bottom. The boots fit loosely. He tied pieces of rope around their tops. He grabbed his only worldly possessions—his sack of borrowed books. The owners of the books would likely refer to them as "stolen", but Simon had every intention of returning them one day. He fled the cave.

Simon lost one boot. When he doubled back to find it, he heard someone yell.

"He was here! He was in this cave!"

Simon swore to himself. That was one more hideout he could no longer trust. That list was growing too long.

The people of the kingdom figured out the secret of the full moon a year ago.

They had found him again.

Simon was about to give up when he spotted the shank of the boot. He grabbed it on the run. The hunters were far too close for him to take the time to put the boot on, so he held it against his chest as he made his way toward the tree-line. He had flown over this mountain many times in the dead of night and he knew it well. Unfortunately, his bare feet were now all-too human. He clenched his teeth together and ignored the pain. He planned to use the rock-face on this side of the mountain to avoid being tracked. This tactic had saved his skin more than once.

He heard the sounds of pursuit behind him. Simon knew that many others had heard the horns and were on their way. He scrambled into the rocks and ran parallel to the tree-line.

"I see him! Above the trees! Look at the moon!" the shouting came from below him.

Simon looked up. The full moon was behind him—providing the perfect backdrop for his silhouette.

"Is your only purpose to curse me?" Simon said to the night sky. He turned to run again, but he stepped into a pile of loose stones. His right leg shot out from under him and he began to slide. Simon fought back a cry when his ankle twisted. He dropped the boot again. A strong hand grabbed his wrist.

It is finally over. Simon closed his eyes.

"Lousy time for a nap, Mate," a voice said.

"Boone," Simon said. "I had given up on you."

"I can't blame you, there," Boone said. "I was a member of this hunting party 'til an hour ago. I had to knock out two of my neighbors to get here."

Boone pulled Simon to his feet. He gave him the boot.

"There are horses tied up less than a mile from here. We'd best be moving. They could come from all directions now."

Simon and Boone abandoned the rock-face and fled into the trees. There was no more reason to be quiet. They halted when they heard the unmistakable sound of hounds in the distance.

"They're getting better at this," Simon said.

"You bet they are," Boone said. "Every man in the Kingdom wants your head. And you have this nasty little habit of screaming and blowing flames into the air."

"Tell me about the Witch," Simon said as they dodged among the trees.

"Lady Magdalena was still—" Boone said.

"She's no lady," Simon spat. "And I'll have worse names for her than 'witch' when I get my hands around her neck. Will they still have her under the watch of the King's Guard?"

"They're posting only two or three of late," Boone said, breathing heavily. "They believe you're no longer a threat and that they're close to catching you. There are the horses. Hurry!"

Boone and Simon untied the reins. They mounted the horses as arrows flew past their heads. The hounds drew nearer. The men leaned against their horse's necks and let them find their own way through the dense forest. The sounds of the hunting party grew faint and distant. The forest gave way to patches of green fields, and small running streams. The horses slowed and drank. Boone and Simon heard the dogs closing in again from two directions.

"We can't let them surround us or we're done for," Boone said.

"How close are we to the main road?" Simon asked.

An arrow struck a tree next to Simon's head.

"Not close enough," Boone said. He pointed back up the mountainside.

"We should go back into the trees."

Once again they put distance between themselves and the hunters. The horses continued to weave through the trees until the forest grew sparser. Simon saw smoke in the distance. They were nearing the village. He breathed a sigh of relief.

"We're almost there, old frien—"

An arrow thrummed past Simon's head and pierced Boone's horse. A moment later, Boone cried out in pain. He clutched his side, and the quill of an arrow. His horse fell.

"NO!" Simon yelled.

Simon jumped to the ground. The hunters were closing in.

"Simon," Boone whispered. "I'm shot."

"I see that," Simon said. "But you'll have to help me get you on my horse—or we're both dead."

"Go. I'm done for."

"Hold your tongue. I'm not leaving my only friend in the world to this bunch."

Boone looked down at his blood-soaked hand.

"I don't think a Healer can save me, Simon."

"No," Simon said. "We'll need magic this night."

The ground rumbled beneath them.

"We may have magic with us, after all," Boone said.

Simon's horse lowered itself to the ground. The horse nuzzled his companion as the wounded horse breathed its last. Simon hurried to help Boone onto his horse's back.

They reached a fast-running river without seeing more arrows. The horse tried to take them into the water. Simon pulled on the reins.

"The river is too deep here, Boy. Let's find shallow water."

The horse was insistent. It plunged them into the deep water and quickly covered a great distance. They heard no more sounds from the hunters. Simon patted the horse's side.

"I'm sorry I doubted your judgment, my good fellow. It won't happen again."

FIVE

The late night was silent except for the occasional distant wolf howl, barking dog, or whinny from a restless horse. Simon supported most of Boone's weight while Boone continued to bleed. They stopped in the shadows of a dwelling; the home of the Sorceress, Magdalena.

"It is true, then," Simon whispered. "Her home is clad in the King's steel."

He rapped the wall with his knuckles.

"I suppose I should feel honored."

"Aye," Boone grimaced. "I see but two guards— and they are prepared for nothing, except to sleep."

"I'll have to lower you to the ground, my friend," Simon whispered. "Are you ready?"

Boone nodded. He whimpered and moaned as Simon lowered him to his backside. He exhaled and leaned against the wall.

"I am sorry, Simon. We were supposed to steal more books tonight—and I've gone and got myself shot."

"It is not stealing. I only mean to borrow them for a while. Your language skills still need work, but we will worry about that later."

Boone winced and nodded.

"Hold steady, Friend," Simon said. "I'll make quick work of these two."

"Wait," Boone said. "Take my sword. I have no use for it."

Simon showed Boone the farmer's short sword.

"I'm better off with this," Simon said. "I had one just like it in the days of—when I was just a boy."

"Where did you get that hideous thing? From some wash-woman?"

"That's not a bad guess."

Simon crept to the corner of the house. He picked up a stone and threw it into the trees. The guards straightened up. One of them crept toward the edge of the woods. The other stayed and guarded the entrance.

Simon hugged the wall of the house and held the short sword in front of him. He grabbed the guard at the door around the head—covering his mouth. Simon meant to whisper in the man's ear to be silent, but the man bit down on his hand. Simon cried out in surprise and pain. The guard's last decision had sealed his fate. Simon closed his eyes, clenched his teeth, and drove the blade into the guard's back.

"Look out, Simon!" Boone said, weakly.

The other guard ran to his partner's aid. He raised his sword over his head. He paused when he heard Boone's cry.

"Simon?" the guard said.

His mouth was still open when the dagger flew

into it. The guard crumpled to the ground.

The dagger throw took the last of Boone's strength. He toppled to his side—snapping the shaft of the arrow.

Simon slapped Boone's face and begged him to wake up, to no avail.

Simon stood. He walked to the door and stood to the side. He banged his fist against it. He flexed his fingers as he heard the door latch operate. A woman's head appeared.

Simon's long-time dream came true.

His fingers squeezed the neck of the sorceress who had cursed him.

Lady Magdalena fought against Simon as he pushed her inside the house. He shoved her into a chair and pulled a length of rope from his waist. Magdalena continued to struggle. Simon held her arms and looked about the room.

"I do not intend to hurt you. I need you alive. But I notice that the inside of your home is still quite....vulnerable. Quite... flammable. You do not want me to be here when tomorrow's moon rises."

"What do you want?" Magdalena spat.

Simon chuckled.

"I want many things—but not on this night!"

Simon continued to bind the woman to the chair.

"What do you think I can do while bound to a chair? Sing for you?"

"I have to go get something," Simon said. "And I,

of all people, know you cannot be trusted."

"If you've killed my guards, you have little time to accomplish anything. We both know you won't kill me — your curse is bound to me."

Simon leaned close to Magdalena's face. She turned away.

"It is true. I have considerable restraint while in my human form, My Lady. But remember this — countless days and nights I have shivered in an empty darkness. There have been nights when my hunger is so strong that nothing matters to me more than my next meal. In those moments, while my body regains strength by consuming another's flesh — when my thoughts grow still and I am aware of the innocent blood that drips from my mouth onto the cold ground —

"In those moments, my foul mood knows no limits and I yearn for death.

"In those moments, I could snap your neck without a second thought, and then plunge myself into the deepest sea."

Simon dragged Boone through the door and laid him on the floor in front of the sorceress.

"You will help him, or at the next moon we shall fly to Valhalla together."

"Untie me," Magdalena said. "Get him on the table and strip him."

Simon drew Boone's sword. He stared at Magdalena as he leaned the sword against the hearth. He untied her. Magdalena examined Boone's wound.

"Don't even think about—"

Magdalena did not look up.

"I possess an outstanding memory. I have not forgotten your threats. Right now, I need for you to be quiet."

Magdalena gathered containers from her cupboard and sprinkled them into a cauldron. She chanted unintelligible words. Boone stirred and moaned.

"Open his mouth," Magdalena said.

Simon lifted Boone's head with one hand. He spread Boone's jaws open with the other. Magdalena poured liquid from a cup down Boone's throat while she continued to chant. Boone swallowed. He coughed. He began to shake.

"Hold onto him," Magdalena said. "There will be a great deal of pain."

Simon held Boone's hands and laid his weight across him. His face was inches from the shaft of the arrow. Magdalena resumed her chants. They became quicker and louder.

The sorceress dipped a ladle into the steaming cauldron. She held it above Boone's side and poured. Her chants became shouts. The liquid sizzled as it hit Boone's flesh. His back arched in agony. He screamed and bucked against Simon's grip. It was all Simon could do to keep Boone on the table.

SIX

Simon struggled to breathe. Blood ran down the length of his forearms where Boone clawed at him. The smear of blood made holding Boone even more difficult.

Boone bucked against Simon's grip until he grew weak. Magdalena continued to chant. She refilled the ladle and poured again.

Boone quivered under Simon's grip. The end of the arrow shaft vibrated. Its movements became more intense until it was moving too fast to see. Boone cried silently and tears rolled down his cheeks. He was too exhausted to scream or to buck any more.

Simon could not take his eyes from the arrow. The skin on Boone's side glowed red. White, oily smoke poured from the hole in his side.

The shaft of the arrow grew longer. It grew longer still. It grew to the length of a man's hand until the edge of the arrowhead appeared. When the widest of the arrowhead exited Boone's body, he arched his back and screamed. He fell back to the table, unconscious.

The arrow clattered to the floor.

Magdalena stumbled back to the chair and fell into

it. Simon put his hand across Boone's chest. He felt his friend's heart beating strong.

"Will he live?"

Magdalena laughed.

"Of course, he will live—as surely as you will continue to cross the sky save for one damnable night at the full moon. You have somehow managed to make one friend. How did you accomplish this?"

"Do not think you have earned the right to interrogate me, Witch."

Magdalena dismissed the remark with a wave of her hand.

"I have been called every foul name in six different tongues, Son of Bailin. Do not think—"

Simon whipped the sword toward Magdalena's neck.

"Never address me that way again."

Magdalena lifted one hand and placed a finger against the tip of the sword. She pushed it away.

"As you wish, Simon—the would-be King. We have an understanding. No more name-calling."

Boone moaned and stirred, but remained unconscious.

"You have done an admirable thing," Magdalena said. "To trade one's life for another is indeed the noblest of sacrifices."

"I have no intention of dying anytime soon."

"I must disagree. No one has seen you for many years. Everyone assumed you were dead. Sterling stopped sending out search parties after only a few months. It is true that those men had little desire to find you. Your legend grew much more frightening in your absence.

"Had you remained in the mountains and the caves, you would likely have been able to live to a ripe old dragon age. But you flaunted yourself in full view — stealing dead animals from hunters. Are these the actions of an intelligent creature? I think not!

"Tonight, you have murdered two soldiers of the King's Guard. Well, I certainly hope you've murdered them."

"What is that supposed to mean?"

A look of revelation crossed Magdalena's face. Her smile was wicked and knowing.

"Have you learned nothing of your dear brother's reign—from the throne that would have been yours?"

She pointed at Boone.

"Your friend must bring you no news from the village."

"Our lives are not your concern. Yes, the guards are dead. I meant to leave them alive, but they left us no choice."

"You did them a great favor," Magdalena said.

"Favor? Are you mad?"

Magdalena leaned forward. Her face grew hard.

"Are you familiar with the role of the King's Regent?" Magdalena asked. "Do you know who rules the Kingdom?"

"Of course," Simon said. "I learned the line of Kings and the laws of succession before my fifth name day. When a young boy becomes King, all matters of the Kingdom are subject to the rule of the Regent."

"Then you know the Kingdom is currently under the rule of your uncle, until your brother's seventeenth name day," Magdalena said.

"That is the law," Simon said.

"Ha! It is the law! And naturally, the law provides the very best for the people of Morgenwraithe! All hail The Law!"

"So, you think little of the laws of the Kingdom," Simon said. "I am not surprised. Your black magic brought about this plague! This is why your guards died. And in your madness, you declare that I have done them a great favor!"

"The fate of my guards was sealed the moment you touched my door. If they lived, Lord Sterling, in your brother's name, would bind them in the center of his courtyard and force them to watch as their families were murdered. He would take their heads and mount them high above the city gates until the crows devoured the last of their flesh."

Simon stepped backward. He leaned against the table. He put his hand on Boone's chest and felt it beating.

"You are lying," Simon said, but he was unable to look at the sorceress.

"I have no reason to lie. And you are no more a prisoner than I am—except that my imprisonment gains no respite from the moon."

"Is there no end to your deceit?" Simon asked. "You are no man's prisoner. Neither the King nor any of his men possess any magic. They would have no need for sorcery or seers if they did."

Magdalena sighed.

"If this was true, I would have fled this Kingdom long ago. Either you toy with me, or you do not know of the unbreakable spell that was placed on the throne of this Kingdom—many, many years ago. No magic can be used against the throne."

"I heard this fable—even as a child. I did not believe it. What kind of magic cannot be broken?"

"I doubt anyone told you the entire story," Magdalena said. "It is not the kind of story that one tells to children."

"Enlighten me," Simon said.

"These lands have known war for as long as anyone can remember. Those who acquired the throne were forever in danger from usurpers—particularly usurpers with sorcerers at their side. This went on for many years until the reign of King Vehaillion—the King from whom—"

"Vehaillion was the first King of—"

"Do not interrupt me!" Magdalena screamed. "I am quite aware of the succession of Kings! And I know

about the dark magic that poisons their bloodline —
something you know nothing about!"

Simon scowled, but remained silent.

"The people of Vehallion's time referred to him as
'Vehaillion the Cruel' or just 'The Cruel One' — not
outside of private circles, of course. More than a few lost
their heads from loose tongues."

"What does this have to do with unbreakable
magic? The more you speak, the less I trust you."

Magdalena stood. Simon raised his sword.

"What are you doing?"

Boone cried out. Simon turned and saw his friend
spasm in pain, his back arched off of the table.
Magdalena brushed past Simon and took the ladle from
the cauldron. She muttered more words as she poured.

"How long before he is well and able to travel?"
Simon asked.

"You should have time to run me through with
your sword and make your escape before the guards are
discovered," Magdalena said.

"And live as a dragon for the rest of my days? I
think not."

Magdalena stood in front of Simon and stared
deep into his eyes.

"You have just answered your own question."

"What does that mean?" Simon asked.

"The blood seal. The truth of unbreakable magic.

"King Vehaillion learned that an attack was being

raised against him by a lord from across the sea. This young lord enlisted the aid of an old and powerful wizard. Vehaillion laid a trap for them on the coast of Islemar.

"Vehaillion captured the lord along with his personal guard. Fifty men were executed in the throne room at Morgenwraithe. Vehaillion bound the invading lord. He forced him to watch as he tortured his wizard. He commanded the wizard to place a spell of protection on the throne of Morgenwraithe. When this was done, King Vehaillion forced the wizard onto his knees in front of the throne. He drew his own dagger and slit the wizard's throat. The wizard's life and blood spilled onto the throne and sealed the spell for all time."

Simon found it difficult to breathe.

"How do I know this to be true?" he asked.

"Perhaps because you witnessed the madness surrounding the throne. Perhaps because you saw the power and madness exhibited by your own parents. The dark spell that was sealed in blood reaches far beyond protection of the throne. Such a powerful curse carries many layers of poison! Why should anyone believe that King Simon would have escaped its influence?"

"I was only a child—"

"Spare me the lies of your innocence!" Magdalena yelled.

Her eyes blazed with a sudden fury. Simon took a step back and readied his sword. Magdalena waved her hand in the air. The sword glowed red hot. Simon screamed and opened his hand. The sword clattered to the floor and flew against a far wall.

"If you pick that up again, be prepared to use it!" Magdalena said. "Seal your fate forever with my blood, if you dare! Perhaps you would find that easier than hearing the truth.

"You know nothing, Boy! A man who will not use his ears to learn is no man at all. You may as well bear your father's name."

Simon stepped toward the sorceress. He pushed a finger behind each of his ears.

"You speak of 'the truth' as if you value its importance. The truth means everything to me. If you speak the truth, I will listen."

SEVEN

"What do you remember?" Magdalena asked. "We will see if time has softened your memory."

"I was only a child," Simon said. "I saw you in the castle almost every day."

"Naturally. I was your father's seer."

"No, Arienna was father's seer," Simon said.

Magdalena barked a laugh.

"That's right! I was replaced as your father's seer—by my own daughter! My daughter—and your cousin."

"My cousin? Is this another of your tricks?"

"Lord Sterling Morgenwraithe," Magdalena spit out the name.

"What about him?"

"He raped me! When I was only a child! And for long enough afterward that his baby grew inside of me."

Simon said nothing.

"When the child swelled in my belly, I thought it a blessing, at first. Sterling grew tired of me. To this day, he has few interests beyond strong drink and bedding every woman in the village. His central mission is spreading hate and fear throughout the land by using your brother's reign to spread his vile poison."

"I only knew Lucien as a baby," Simon whispered. "A beautiful and innocent baby."

"To Lord Sterling, your brother has been nothing but a tool—his own means by which to rule."

Simon raised a shaking hand.

"You blame the woes of the Kingdom on everyone but yourself! In this very instant, I could choke the life from you! I have dreamed of it. You tell tales of all the evil that has befallen this kingdom in the wake of your curse—as if you were not the one responsible! I was to have been the King! I would never have—!"

"You would never have lived to become King, you stupid, stupid, boy!" Magdalena cried.

Simon balled his fists.

"How dare you say such a thing?" Simon yelled.

"I was there, the day you were born," Magdalena said. "Your father named you, without ever asking your mother. Do you know why he chose the name Simon?"

"What difference does that make?"

"Simon is not the name of any King! It was the name of a court jester—the same one that your father and his brother called to entertain them when they were drunk."

"What does that matter? I would still have become the Kin—"

"No, you would not," Magdalena said.

"Most Kings would be thrilled with the arrival of a strong, healthy son. But not your father! In you, he saw his own frail humanity. He foresaw the day he would grow weak and unable to rise from his bed. He foresaw the day you would step in and take his power away from him.

"Your birth only fueled his wish to achieve immortality—at any cost!"

"This makes a fascinating story," Simon said. "But why should you know of it? Were you in the King's confidence?"

Magdalena laughed.

"Who do you think he charged with discovering the dark magic of immortality? Who was forced to spend their every waking hour in the quest for the darkest of secrets? Only I was charged with gaining the means for the Mad King to live forever!"

"But you failed," Simon said. "I was there to see that. Of course, at the same time I should have become King, I became a Beast. One way or the other, Father got his wish."

"It's true he hated you—in the beginning. But you walked across the floor and into his arms within days of learning to crawl. You learned language quickly. The wisest men and women in the Kingdom marveled at your speech—and your abilities to read and to write. You were a favorite among those who cared for you. You managed to melt your father's cold heart.

"Many times, I watched him with you, and I saw a

side of him that no one knew existed. Unfortunately, the more your father loved you, the more obsessed and mad your mother became."

"I do not understand. Why should my mother resent the bonding between a father and his son?"

"There was no logic to her madness! I believe it sprang from the wizard's curse and was fueled by her hatred of your father's wandering eye. This is where our lives converge, my would-be King."

Boone stirred again, but only briefly. He snored.

"Go on," Simon said.

"I knew Arienna had many gifts—the same as I had," Magdalena said. "I did everything I could to keep these secret. She was so pure and beautiful—I feared that Sterling would lust after her. But what happened was even worse. Her beauty captured the eye of your father. He sensed that she possessed the gifts of magic. Your father sat Arienna before him and tricked her with questions about the future.

"He moved her into the castle on the same day he moved me out. Arienna soon told me that the King visited her in her chambers. It was not long before your mother found out. That was when she came to see me."

"Do not think I hold my mother and father blameless," Simon said. "I saw their madness with my own eyes."

"But there is much that you could not know. The Queen burned with rage—and the rage never subsided. It grew with each passing day. Her madness was not of this earth.

"It is true that I hated the King for taking my child away from me. He was ruining her mind and body with his filthy adultery. I no longer cared if I lived or died as long as I could destroy him. But I was powerless. In my desperation and anguish, I told all this to the Queen. She offered me vengeance—if I agreed to provide her with the same."

"You conspired with her to destroy my entire family," Simon said.

"No!" Magdalena said. "No. Your mother betrayed me."

Simon stared.

"My sixth name day. I was to be introduced to the people as the heir to the throne. Such a magnificent day—bright and sunny. Father addressed the people from the balcony. Arienna stood behind him. Father turned and said, 'Join me, my Queen'.

"My mother stepped behind Arienna and grabbed her by the hair. She pulled a dagger and sliced Arienna's throat. My father ran toward them, but Mother plunged the dagger into his chest.

"I watched my mother take her own life—while you placed your curse upon me. She screamed as she died—

"Behold! Your new King!'"

"The bitch deserved a thousand deaths!"

Magdalena cried. "She murdered my beautiful daughter! Slaughtered her like a pig! My beautiful, innocent Arienna!"

Simon sank onto a bench.

"The King's Guard ran at me—screaming, and waving torches and swords. I didn't know what was happening—but I knew I was going to die.

"I threw myself from the balcony. I was six years old. I was alone, and hurt, and I was….

"A dragon."

Boone moaned in his sleep. Simon crossed the floor and looked at the wound in Boone's side. The wound was closed, and the only sign of the arrow's entry was a ring of red skin.

"He will wake soon," Magdalena said.

"You are coming with us," Simon said.

"To where?"

"I will hear everything—everything you know. You have nothing to fear from me. Our futures are intertwined."

"I need to visit the privy," Magdalena said.

Simon scowled.

"What?" Magdalena scowled, as well. "Do you think a sorceress does not void herself? Are you that baffled by magic?"

"I will have to come with you."

"Of course. Bring your sword if it will make you feel better."

"Don't worry. I will."

Simon followed Magdalena. He grabbed her by the arm as his eyes swept across the garden.

Simon opened the door to the privy. He pushed against each board with the tip of his sword.

"Be quick about it," he said. He let go of her arm.

He held the door open and turned away.

"You cannot be serious," Magdalena said. "This is humiliating!"

"Very well. But I shall be right here, with the tip of my sword at the height of your neck. Do not try my patience."

Simon tapped his toe and counted to twenty.

"I'm opening the door now. That should have been long enou—"

The privy was empty.

Simon looked and looked for every conceivable way that the sorceress might have escaped, but he knew the answer to that question.

The privy was bewitched. Simon felt like a fool.

He hung his head.

Simon heard a voice from the back doorway of Magdalena's house. Boone slumped there against the door frame.

"What have I missed?"

EIGHT

A cock crowed as Simon and Boone searched Magdalena's bedroom.

"We need to get out of here," Boone said. "When the guards fail to report in, this place will be swarming with the King's men."

"I know," Simon said. He grabbed hold of a bag beneath the mattress. He dumped the contents onto the bed.

"What are these?" Simon asked.

Boone picked up a piece.

"This is a copper."

He sifted through the coins.

"That is a silver. Those three are gold."

"How much does a suit of man's clothing cost?" Simon asked.

"You mean, like a suit for a wedding? Or a burial?"

"No," Simon said. "Clothes for working. Trousers and a shirt. And a pair of boots."

"You mean to go shopping? Surely you don't mean to do this today."

"How much?" Simon repeated.

"Ten coppers. No, you'd better make that fifteen, with the boots."

"How many coppers to a silver then?"

"A silver?" Boone said. He struggled to count in his head.

"About fifty coppers to a silver I think."

Simon nodded. He put one silver coin in his pocket and put the rest back into the sack.

"Why not take it all?" Boone asked. "Throw it down the privy, if nothing else. The witch stole your life from you."

"I hope to one day be your King, my friend. Is that the actions of a King?"

"A real King, no. The one we have now, who knows?"

Boone picked up the sack. He pocketed a silver coin and then put the sack back under the mattress.

"I see that you have no such reservations," Simon said.

"After tonight, there will be a bounty on my head, as well. I've heard whispers that a wizard from across the sea has set up shop in the market. He sells a type of magic called 'spyglass'."

"Spyglass? What is that?"

"A hollow stick. The stick holds a type of magic that makes far away things look like they're right in front of you. Something like that might save our skins for one more day."

"I should have asked the witch more questions

about our dear King Lucien," Simon said.

"All I know about your brother are the rumors told by old women," Boone said. "Even the drunkards in the pubs know better than to speak ill of the King. He has eyes and ears all around the village. I have heard there is a bounty for information about any who would disrespect or be a threat to the throne. And you wonder why I stay to the woods and the mountains! I should have become the dragon."

The cock crowed again.

Simon and Boone ran into what remained of the night.

Just before dawn, Simon and Boone lay waiting near the road into the village. When the first of the traders' wagons rolled past, they fell in behind them — just another pair of traveling merchants.

Their faces were unknown — other than by the sorceress.

They passed by only two of the King's Guard at the walls surrounding the village.

"They haven't fortified the entry," Boone whispered. "Nor does it seem that they are on watch for strangers."

"If I didn't know better, I would think you were disappointed," Simon whispered.

"Surprise is not disappointment, Your Majesty," Boone said.

Simon elbowed Boone in his side.

"Be careful with your words, Boone. Such

references are far too dangerous. If someone were to hear you, we could be surrounded within moments—and this day would prove to be our last."

"Sorry," Boone said. "Since you're the smart one—tell me again why we're inside the village, and where we're going."

"I need to relearn the layout of the village and the castle if I'm ever to make this place my own," Simon said. "I doubt Magdalena has yet taken her story to the King. She will think of a way to use the information to her advantage. She is no fool."

Boone studied Simon's face.

"I am curious about the conversation the two of you had, standing above me while I nearly died," Boone said. "It is as if you have gained respect for the witch! If you are mistaken, and she has already informed Lord Sterling, today could be the end of us. You might never sprout wing again."

"What if that was the end I sought, Boone? For an end to my cursed existence?"

"You don't frighten me," Boone spat on the ground.

"If I die at the side of my rightful King, then my life is not wasted. It is fulfilled!"

"Well said, but let us be quiet. We are within the hearing of the castle's little birds."

Simon and Boone stood in front of the castle gates. They heard the carrion cries above their heads. They looked up.

A row of vertical iron spikes displayed three human heads. Crows fought each other and picked at the few remains of flesh that clung to the skulls.

Simon and Boone stared silently at the horrible sight.

"So, you come to gloat—and sing the praises of your kingdom!" said the voice behind them.

Simon and Boone jumped. They pulled their cloaks up high on their necks. Boone stepped in front of Simon and turned. A young maid glared at him. She carried a basket of fruit.

"No, My Lady," Boone said. "We are strangers to your village. It is our first trip here, aboard a merchant vessel."

"You needn't address me as 'My Lady'," the girl said. "I am only a handmaid. Handmaid to the Queen. My uncle was a sea merchant. I traveled with him once. What village are you from?"

Boone swallowed hard. He looked to Simon.

"Privea," Simon said.

Boone covered his laugh with a cough.

"We have only just arrived," Simon said. "We mean no disrespect. Who...did you know these men?"

"Do you swear that you are not spies?" the young maid whispered. "Sent by the King?"

"No," Simon said softly. "Please believe me. We bend the knee to no King."

The girl smiled.

"My uncle always said his only King had a wooden deck and sailed the high seas."

"He is a wise man," Boone said. "I would like to meet him."

The girl's smile faded.

She pointed up.

"My two uncles. And my father."

"I'm sorry," Simon said.

"They were men of peace—even to the end, when peace became useless," the young lady spoke as if in a trance. "Lord Sterling has convinced the King that every surrounding province is a threat to his sovereignty. One by one, the King's armies overrun the villages. So many innocent have been slaughtered or enslaved—the men are killed—and the old women. The young women and children are forced into labor. Or worse."

"You are quite free with your stories—told to complete strangers," Boone said.

"They have taken everything from me," the girl said. "The only thing left to use against me is the fear of death. So, I try not to fear it."

Simon could not take his eyes off of the beautiful young girl. The sun illuminated the side of her face and he saw the bruise under her eye.

"Who struck you?" he asked.

The young maid looked around in all directions.

"Helena! Come, child!" An old woman yelled and waved at the young maid.

The girl looked frightened. She turned to Simon and Boone.

"You must not ask such things!" she screamed in a whisper. "His spies are everywhere!"

She turned and ran through the gates. Three apples toppled from her basket.

Simon and Boone watched after her, and then Simon stooped and picked up the apples. He handed one to Boone.

"Two for you and one for me," Boone said. "I see how it is."

Simon closed one eye and peered into the sky.

"In a few hours I will put on about two thousand pounds."

"I forgot about that. You do eat like a pig."

"Ah, a pig," Simon sighed. "Two pigs would be even better!"

"Making demands for your dinner, now, are you?" Boone said. "I'd be tempted to call you a spoiled bastard, except when you take the throne you'll have my head on one of your spikes!"

Simon laughed for a moment, but then a small piece of rotted flesh hit the ground in front of him, and his face became like stone. He squinted up into the empty eye sockets of the three men he would never know.

They were more than likely guilty of nothing, Simon thought. Those men should be laughing and bouncing grandchildren upon their laps. And they would be—

If King Simon ruled these lands.

"I'll have no heads up there," Simon said. "I may plant flowers, instead."

Simon clapped Boone on the shoulder.

"If I become King, you will be at my side. You will be required to call me at least one insulting name per day—lest I forget my place."

Boone looked toward the castle.

"That was a lovely girl."

"Yes," Simon said. "Almost the loveliest I have ever seen."

"Oh? What young lady have you seen who is lovelier than that? I would like to look upon her, myself."

"We have more important things to do this day than ogle young ladies," Simon said.

"Hopefully, this lovely girl did not pay so much attention to us," Boone said.

"You heard her story, the same as I," Simon said. "She may try not to fear death, but she is surrounded by it. Who in the village would she confide in?"

NINE

Lord Sterling stood at the second-story balcony. He squinted and shaded his eyes from the bright sunshine. When he saw the Queen's maid approaching, he walked down to meet her.

"You. Girl," he said.

The girl bowed her head.

"Yes, Lord Sterling."

"Those two men—at the gate," he purred. "You spoke to them. Who are they? What was said?"

"They were looking for the market," she said.

"The market," Lord Sterling scowled. "They are strangers?"

"Yes, My Lord. Sea merchants."

"What are you called, again?"

The girl dipped her knees in a slight curtsy.

"Helena, My Lord."

"Helena," Lord Sterling repeated. He drew back his right hand.

"You would not dare to lie to the King's Regent, would you?"

Helena began to cry.

"No, my Lord."

Sterling reached toward Helena. She flinched and turned her head aside.

Sterling grabbed the locket that lay against her chest.

"Why does a servant girl have a trinket about her neck?"

"Please, My Lord. My mother gave it to me. The Queen says I may keep it."

A shadow appeared by Sterling's side. He looked over his shoulder. The King stood above him on the balcony.

Sterling let the locket fall.

"I will speak to the King about this," Sterling snapped. "Allowing servants to wear jewelry? What is next? Servants dining at our tables?"

"No, My Lord," Helena said. "It is just...it is all I have to remind me of my family."

"Ha!" Sterling barked. "I will see that the skulls are brought to you—when the crows are finished with them!"

Sterling lowered his hand and took Helena by the arm.

"I do not believe your story," he whispered in Helena's ear. "As I believed none of your people's claims of loyalty to the throne. But I'll not strike you again."

Sterling smiled wickedly.

"I do believe that our young King fancies a certain young maid. You should make splendid sport."

Sterling walked with Helena until they were out of the King's view. He slung her to the ground. The basket of fruit spilled in every direction.

"Do not dare to bring bruised fruit to our table. Go and fill the basket again."

Sterling walked away.

TEN

Boone looked up to the sun, which was directly overhead.

"Have you seen enough?" Boone asked. "We should not be seen lurking here in the light of day. No one knows our faces—and that will forever be our best defense. We certainly cannot risk being seen by the witch."

"The 'Witch' saved your life, Boone," Simon said.

Boone placed a hand on his side without thinking.

"Aye. But without her damned curse, I would be rocking on the porch and puffing my pipe under the light of the moon, instead of thrashing bareback down a mountainside."

"Let's be off, then," Simon said. He took the silver coin from his pocket.

"Only one task remaining, and then we can leave the village."

Boone shook his head slowly.

"I can't believe you dare to risk having more villagers see us," Boone said. "We'll have to cross through half the town to get to the market. There could be dozens of people there at midday."

"As you said, Boone, our faces are unknown. And look around you — the people keep their eyes cast upon the ground. It was the same in my father's day."

"True, those in the streets hope to bring themselves no attention, and cast no shadow. But you've heard of the bounties. No doubt there are eyes around every corner — waiting to gain the King's favor by making up tales about suspicious-looking strangers. The rule of the day is to torture and execute first and ask questions later. I would wager that Sterling asked very few questions of those men on the wall."

Boone leaned close to Simon's ear.

"The man who could capture you in human flesh would never toil another day in his life."

Simon ignored Boone and continued to walk. At a street corner, they walked by an old man who was drunk and passed out — even at midday. His battered old hat had fallen off of his head and lay beside him in the dirt. Simon plucked it from the ground without stopping. He put the hat on his head and pulled it low over his eyes.

"There. Now, I am in deep disguise."
Boone chuckled.
"Oh, sure. You won't take a few coins from the Witch, but you take an old fool's hat."
"I'll bring it back before we leave," Simon said.
Boone pushed Simon.
"Like hell, you will."

They avoided the most crowded streets, taking a circuitous route to the market. When they left the shops, the sun faded toward the forest.

"Which direction is your home?" Simon asked.

"West," Boone pointed.

"We should leave the village the opposite way," Simon said. "I'll take you home tonight—after we've rested."

Boone grimaced and clutched at his side. Simon grabbed Boone's arm.

"What's wrong?" Simon asked. He raised Boone's shirt, fearing the worst.

The wound remained closed, marked only by a tinge of red skin.

"There's still healing to be done," Boone said. "It feels like there are tiny men at work in there—using tiny spades and hammers to patch my insides back together."

"We'll be safe, and clear of the city in just a little while, mate," Simon said. "There's no need to push on— it wouldn't do for your wound to open up. We have no more help left."

They walked away from the village for two hours. Three times Simon asked Boone if they should stop. Boone shook his head each time. They pushed through dense brush to a cave that remained one of Simon's safe havens.

"There is a stream not far from here," Simon said.

"Let's push on, then," Boone said.

They came to the stream and drank their fill.

Simon fell back on the ground. Boone took off his shirt and rinsed off the dirt and sweat. Simon sat up.

He could see the welts on Boone's back in the very last rays of sunlight.

"Your father—he still beats you?"

"Only when he's drunk," Boone said, as he wrung out his shirt. He pulled it on quickly.

"Every day, then, is what you mean."

"It used to be twice a day," Boone attempted a smile. "But he grows old, and tired."

"But, still—"

"Look, Simon. When he hits me, he's not hitting Mother—and she's not doing so well anymore. She's not much help in the fields, as it is."

"You're a good man, Boone. You should not have to live this way."

Boone laughed.

"Look who's talking about the right way to live— my Dragon-King!"

They shared a laugh and a handshake.

They walked back to the cave. Simon pointed to the nest he had built some months ago.

"There you are, my friend. Nothing but the finest accommodations."

"I need not take your bed," Boone said. "At this moment I could sleep hanging upside down in a tree."

"You should rest," Simon said. "It will be safer if we travel after midnight. I need no sleep." Simon looked into the twilight outside the mouth of the cave.

"It is almost time."

"You still wish for me to stay away?" Boone asked.

"I understand that you find it fascinating," Simon said. "But the thought of you watching frightens me."

Boone laughed.

"You? Frightened? You took down a King's Guard! You commanded the services of the most powerful sorceress in the land—at the point of a sword!"

Simon looked sad.

"You are my only friend. In my eyes, your bravery knows no equal. You helped me when I could not help myself. But the transformation is a curse—at the full moon, and the night after. I have no desire for you to regard me differently."

"You are my only friend, as well," Boone said. "There is nothing that can change that."

"Please, Boone," Simon said.

Boone walked to the edge of the makeshift bed.

"As you wish, my King."

Boone lay down on the bed and was asleep within seconds.

Simon leaned against the cave wall. He closed his eyes and dozed.

The beginning twinges in his hands woke him.

Simon scrambled to his feet and ran outside. He breathed in deeply and waited.

The transformation from man to dragon was the opposite experience from the transformation from dragon to man.

Transforming to human was the ultimate in pain. Transforming from human to dragon—

Was pure ecstasy.

In those moments, every stress in Simon's body and mind dissolved into the purest bliss. His mind flooded with colorful visions of green fields, a limitless bounty of mouth-watering meat, and an endless sky. Energy and adrenaline rushed through every ounce of his renewed body. He yearned to fly—He lived to fly. He feared nothing, and he wanted for nothing.

When his transformation was complete, Simon looked into the night sky. He breathed in deeply and exhaled. He was still startled by his first breath of flame after he returned to the body where he spent twenty-nine days out of thirty.

He would fly now. Simon knew it would be wiser to wait, but the drive to spread his wings and eat up the sky was too powerful to resist. This had been a constant since the time of his first transformation—when he had watched his father and mother die by his mother's hand.

He had flown. And flown.

And on every thirtieth day, after twenty-four hours as a man, the dragon had flown. The experience was euphoric, for most of an hour. But when the feelings of freedom subsided, Simon relived the fear and horror of his very first flight as a frightened and cursed Beast.

ELEVEN

When Simon flew back to the cave two hours later, the feeling of euphoria was gone. He looked in on Boone, who was snoring and sleeping deeply.

Simon waited outside the cave. He would let Boone sleep a while longer. Simon heard a rustle in the brush. He looked down and saw a mother rabbit, with three of her young, hop past his talons. He sighed.

Not only was the euphoria of his transformation over, but the feeling he dreaded the most made its presence known.

He was hungry.

Hunger was not new to Simon. He had spent most of his life hungry. By his choice.

There was nothing under the sun that Simon could not capture or kill and devour.

Perhaps, he thought, almost every day of his life — perhaps, if I had never been a boy or a man, I would be a natural killer. If I had been born a dragon, killing might not bother me in the least.

But it did bother him.

"Good evening," Boone said from behind Simon. "Ah, ah, ah! Don't turn around. I'm coming."

Boone walked in front of Simon the dragon.

"Well, here we are again," he sighed.

Simon turned his head and sighed as well. A small burst of flame lit the sky, followed by a trail of black smoke.

Boone laughed.

"I may be your only friend, yet I'll never be able to surprise you. I would become a little pile of ash."

"I'm able to control it, for the most part," Simon said, sadly. "I'm still working on it."

Boone held his arm in front of him and pinched his flesh between his thumb and finger.

"It can take a lot to kill a man. But not when it comes to fire. We can take precious little of that."

"And that is why the dragon has been the most feared creature on earth," Simon said. "The wings and scales, the tail and the jaws, are only decorations compared to the flame."

Simon sat down, shaking the trunks of the trees.

"And that is why it makes the most excellent curse. It is also why the dragons have all but disappeared from the land."

"I remember the last dragon—the one they kept alive," Boone said. "Papa took us to see it. He was drunk. I'll not say how he behaved that day. It was embarrassing."

Simon shook his head and snorted.

"Kept it alive? I was too young to see it, but I heard the tales from the servants. They left the poor creature bound in chains. The people tormented him. They threw stones at him. The children spit upon him. They starved him to the point that he could make no fire. Do you know what happens to the dragon at that point, Boone?"

"No. I only saw it that once, from a distance. I was only a child, but I knew it was not well."

"A dragon with an empty belly is no threat to anyone. Without food, the dragon's belly becomes his greatest enemy. His fire stays within him. The dragon burns—from the inside."

"That is truly awful," Boone said. His face showed pain.

"How did you learn these things?"

"Some of it, I heard from my father's soldiers. And some, I'm learning for myself."

"I heard the dragon's teeth fell out," Boone said.

Simon nodded.

"It's another sign of the empty belly. The dragon dies slowly, and his greatest strength becomes his greatest enemy."

"You need to keep this reality in mind, Simon," Boone said. "What if something happens to me? What if the hunting parties begin to lay in wait for you? You must become a hunter. You are a dragon. You may not like it, but you have little choice."

Simon turned away and breathed harmless fire

into the sky.

"The day that it does not trouble me to take innocent life, is the day I give up my birthright—forever."

"We need to know what Sterling plans to do about the discovery of the dead guards," Boone said. "Who knows what Magdalena will tell him?"

"I do not profess to know," Simon said. "That is why I planned to take her—to determine where her loyalties lie."

"Sterling will do everything in his power to learn what happened," Boone said.

"I hope that he does," Simon said. "In fact, I hope that he pushes her far enough that she snaps his neck."

"I will make every excuse I can to go into the village," Boone said. "Though I doubt that my father will allow it. It is almost time for the harvest, such as it is. I'm old enough now to get into the pubs. I've only been into the village a few times, with my mother. The only thing I ever heard there was women's gossip."

"And we both know men can gossip just as well as the women!" Simon laughed.

"Bite your tongue, Good Sir!" Boone laughed. "Do not dare to speak our secrets aloud! Remember your vows!"

"Consider it done," Simon said. "Forgive me, Minister of the Confidence of Men!"

"We should go," Boone said. "It is late, but we should still stay far away from the village."

"Aye," Simon said. He pushed himself to his feet.
"Wait! Shh!"

Boone held up a hand. He pulled his dagger from
his side and threw it. A large jackrabbit fell over, dead.

"I cannot go home in the middle of the night
empty-handed," Boone said. "What excuse would I
give?"

Simon stared at the rabbit as it twitched its last.

"Will it always bother you, My King?"

"Yes," Simon said. He looked away.

"Were I only a man, I would exist upon carrots
and cabbages. But this body will not allow that. Already,
the hunger cries out from deep in my belly. I will have to
kill before another moon rises."

"Taking back the throne will require much
bloodshed, Simon," Boone said. "You must prepare for it.
A seconds pity may cost a man his life. And an elk or a
deer cannot look you in the eye and ask you 'why?' or
cry out for its mother—"

"Stop it!" Simon roared.

"It will do you no service to withhold the truth,
Simon," Boone said. "If something is not done, and soon,
you may have no choice but to die in that body.
Magdalena disappeared from her privy—she has
magic—but she is also flesh and blood. She is twice your
age, and will not live forever. The sorceress is not as
despised as you are, but she has enemies. Her heart will
not suffer a sword, the same as anyone."

Simon raised his head and snorted another blast of

fire.

"It is difficult to hear, but it is the truth," Simon said.

"That's a pretty big rabbit," Boone said.

Simon laughed.

"You're a good man, Boone Blankenship. Bag your rabbit and let's be off."

TWELVE

"All hail, King Lucien!" came the voice of the crier.

"Hail, King Lucien!" answered the members of the Royal Council and the members of the King's Guard.

Lady Magdalena mouthed the words as well.

The Council gathered to question Magdalena about the night that Simon Morgenwraithe invaded her home and killed two members of the King's Guard.

"It has been quite some time since the Dragon has been seen in his human form," Lord Sterling said. He paced before the throne, holding his ever-present chalice. He stopped and stared at Magdalena.

"What does he look like?"

Magdalena saw Lucien slide to the front of the throne.

The King's obsession with his older brother remains sharp. Smart boy, Magdalena thought.

"He is tall with dark, wavy hair. He is lean and very fit; an imposing figure—and devilishly handsome," Magdalena said.

The Council of Men whispered to one another. Some laughed.

"Silence!" Sterling said. "Do not toy with me, Sorceress. We seek a useful description of the Man-Beast—not your opinion of his ability to turn a woman's mind into porridge!"

Magdalena cleared her throat.

"He looks...like a King."

The murmuring grew louder.

"What did you say?" Sterling growled.

"I am sorry, My Lord. I misspoke," Magdalena said. "I meant to say, he looks like The King. His brother. Only taller...and..."

"And what?" Sterling spat.

"Taller. And...larger."

The murmuring began again. Sterling spun on his heels.

"I will clear this room if you do not stop this incessant chatter! You gossip like a bunch of old spinsters!"

Everyone in the room fell silent.

"What did he say?" Sterling continued.

"As I have already told you, he demanded that I heal the other boy," Magdalena said. "He said if the boy died, then so would I."

"He had to have said more than that!" Sterling said. "Your curse has ruled every minute of his existence. I should imagine he had very much more to say to you!"

"No. He leveled a sword at my neck, and he made threats. That is all—"

"I don't believe you. What are you hiding from us, Sorceress?" Sterling sneered.

Magdalena stood.

"If you wish to supply the answers to your own questions, then I am not needed here."

"I am not finished questioning you," Sterling said. "Sit down."

Magdalena remained standing.

Sterling was outraged.

"I said —!"

"I know exactly what you said, Lord Sterling," Magdalena said. "Perhaps you did not understand my reply! You could ask one of these others here to repeat it for you, but they would be too afraid! In fact, I am the only person in this village who does not fear you whatsoever!"

The room was silent. The men held their breath.

"What more can you do to me?" Magdalena asked. "You had your way with me. You ignored my daughter — your, daughter. You stood by and allowed your own brother to take her when she was still a child. The mad queen forced me to curse one Morgenwraithe — but I have been cursed by every last one of you!"

Sterling grabbed Magdalena's arm. His face was red, and he shook with anger.

"Hold your tongue, Witch! Or I will cut it out and shove it down your throat!"

Sterling jumped back and screamed. His shirt was on fire. Several men helped to put it out.

MY NAME IS SIMON 66

"Your threats are empty, Lord Sterling," Magdalena spat angrily. "I do not fear death—I may even welcome it! But the question that remains—which no one knows the answer to—is...

"If I die, what will become of the dear, sweet Simon Morgenwraithe?"

Magdalena's eyes searched the others in the room. "What say you, Counsel to the King? What will become of the curse in the event of my death? What will happen to the rightful King of the Realm? Nothing? Or will the curse dissolve?"

Everyone looked to Lucien, who now sat against the back of his throne. He looked afraid. He looked ill.

"Ask yourselves, gentlemen, what would happen if the curse no longer existed?"
Magdalena was enjoying herself immensely.
"What if the people became unified behind the rightful King—and demanded he take the throne? Twelve years is a very long time for the new king of the land to plot his revenge against those who have opposed him—"
"That will be all!" Sterling stormed across the floor. "This inquisition is over! Everyone out!"

Sterling watched the last member of the Royal Council leave. Only the Captain of the Guard, two knights, and Lucien remained.

A boy, a very young member of the army, slipped inside the door. He was clearly in a hurry. He was sweating, and nervous.

Sterling got the Captain's attention and motioned him to the corner of the room. The young soldier joined them.

Sterling raised his brow.

"On the night of the full moon, two men were struck on the back of the head, taking them out of the hunt," the young soldier whispered. "Neither of them knows who was responsible."

"What else?" Sterling asked.

The soldier glanced toward the King. The King paid them no attention.

"Two other men say a man—a boy, rather—who was a member of the hunting party—has not been seen since."

"Where does this boy live?" Sterling asked.

The soldier swallowed.

"We are attempting to discover that as we speak, My Lord."

Sterling and the Captain exchanged a look.

"Good," Sterling said. He waved his hand.

"Go. And say nothing to anyone."

"Yes, My Lord. No, My Lord."

The soldier hurried away.

THIRTEEN

"There!" Boone yelled into the wind. "My house is in that clearing ahead!"

Simon skimmed the treetops and landed at the edge of the woods.

"That was incredible!" Boone exclaimed. He stretched his arms and his back.

"It is by far the best part," Simon said. "Don't get used to it."

"I suppose it's an entirely different experience when you're dodging arrows," Boone said.

"And having every foul name under the sun screamed at you at the same time doesn't do much for one's self-esteem," Simon said.

"I'll try to kill a boar, or maybe a deer—if you want to come by tonight," Boone said. "If I get one, I'll leave it right here."

"Thank you, Boone. Be well."

Simon shot into the night sky and disappeared over the trees.

Boone braced himself and turned toward home. He hoped that his father would be more interested in a roasted rabbit than spilling his rage on his only remaining child.

Simon flew to his nearest cave sanctuary. He slept
fitfully, and woke late the next morning. The deep
rumbling of his empty stomach greeted him.

Simon left the cave and walked to the edge of the
cliff that looked down upon a grassy meadow. With his
keen eyes, he saw a herd of deer feeding in the field.

He sighed and looked into the sky. It was too late
in the day to seek a hunting party from which he might
steal a kill.

"For me to live—the innocent must die. And I
wish to lead my people? How many more innocents will
die before my heart turns to stone?"

Simon spread his wings. He looked down on the
herd and tried to see only food, and not life.

"I'm sorry," he said as he launched himself from
the cliff. He circled the meadow to give himself the
broadest expanse of the clearing to give chase. Simon had
no hunting abilities in the thick woods. He flew toward
the herd at top speed. The deer saw the shadow that
alerted them to the dragon's presence. They turned and
ran.

A doe and her two young fawns struggled to keep
pace with the panicked herd. The leader veered to the
north, but the doe and fawns continued toward the
woods that lay due east. Simon closed in on them.

Simon readied himself. He closed his eyes and
inhaled. When he opened his eyes, the doe had stopped

and turned. She stared up at him. The fawns pressed
themselves against their mother's hips. Simon looked
into the doe's eyes—

He pulled up, and away.

Simon continued to climb. He glared into the sun
and refused to blink. He forced himself higher—higher
than he had ever flown.

Can I fly high enough to touch the sun? The
thought went through his mind.

Can I fly high enough to turn these scales to ash—
to end this pointless existence?

Tears streamed from Simon's eyes. He felt no
guilt, and no shame. In that moment, Simon did not care
about anything.

 The air grew thin and cold. Simon bore down
though he found it hard to breathe.

I beg for the heat of the sun to destroy me, yet I
am driven back by the cold, Simon thought as he beat the
thin air with his wings for the last time.

He closed his eyes and turned his head toward the
earth.

I fail again, even at taking my own life. Perhaps
the sorceress saved the Kingdom after all. How could I
possibly lead an entire people?

Simon tucked in his wings and plummeted
toward the earth. The thought passed through his mind
that he could plunge into the rock face of the mountains.
Or, with a slight change of course, he could exhaust his

breath and pierce the depths of the ocean.

But he knew he would do neither.

Simon flew low across the meadow. The deer were gone. No birds sang in the trees, and there was no sign of even the smallest woodland creature. Every living thing feared the hunger of the dragon.

"If they only knew," the dragon said to the emptiness.

The sun was low in the western sky when Simon turned toward Boone's home. His low flight over the forest took a great deal of effort. His belly screamed at him, an early warning. Simon was weak and his wings were heavy.

Please, he thought. Please, my friend. Let there be food at the edge of these woods.

But as Simon neared the Blankenship's farm, he smelled the fire before he saw it. Black smoke rose above the forest. Simon topped a hill and saw a horrific scene— Boone's home was on fire. Worse than that, Simon heard his friend's screams.

"Help!"

Three members of the King's Guard drove their horses hard as they chased Boone along the tree-line. Boone was on foot. Two of the knights held their swords over their heads. The other attempted to line up a shot with his bow.

The smoke burned Simon's eyes. His vision was failing. His belly was relentless in its torture. His belly—

his powerful furnace—was not designed to operate while empty.

"It's the dragon!" one of the knights cried out.

"Simon!" Boone yelled.

Simon dove toward his friend. An arrow whizzed by his head. Knights surrounded him on both sides. Boone would soon be forced into the forest—and Simon could not help him there.

Simon knew he had no choice, and little time. One blast of fire might be all that he could make.

He dove toward the knights at full speed and inhaled. He closed his eyes and felt the fire roil up from his gut and out through his mouth. Simon turned skyward, closed his eyes, and glided—until he no longer heard the men's screams.

Simon stood in the field and watched the roof of the Blankenship home collapse. Boone lay on his back, trying to catch his breath.

"Your parents?" Simon asked.

Boone shook his head. A tear ran down his face.

"The King's Guard was waiting for me."

"I'm sorry," Simon said.

Boone nodded. He sat up and looked around.

"I killed a boar—but it's gone."

Boone pointed and looked at Simon.

"Those horses—they are dead."

Simon stared at the charred animals.

"I must eat, I'm afraid. Could I ask a favor?"

"What is it?" Boone asked.

"Don't watch."

FOURTEEN

Boone pushed himself to his feet. He winced when he tried to put weight on his left leg.

"Are you hurt?" Simon asked.

"I twisted my ankle. It's beginning to stiffen up, that's all."

Night fell quickly. Simon squinted up the hill beyond the ruins of Boone's home. The lights over the hill glowed brighter. More soldiers approached on horseback, carrying torches.

"We have to go," Simon said.

"I'll have to bunk with you—for a while anyway," Boone said. "I have nowhere else to go."

"You can stay with me as long as you want. They will hunt both of us now."

"Please, stop trying to cheer me up," Boone said.

"You are my only friend," Simon said. "And you've lost everything—because of me."

Boone stared at the remains of his family's home.

"I tried to get her to leave with me—to get away from that cruel man. I told her we could make a decent life for ourselves—somewhere far away, where he could never find us. She wouldn't hear of it. 'He is still my husband, and your father!' she would say—as if that meant anything. He broke one of her legs so badly that it never healed right. And one of her hands she could no longer open or close—all at the hand of that bastard. Did I tell you that?"

"No."

Boone sighed.

"I lost very little here today, my friend. The future would have been only more of the same. I hope she has found peace, at long last."

"I am truly sorry," Simon said.

Boone reached as high as he could and put his hand on the dragon's side.

"This day, I trade the life of a poor dirt farmer for the position of Captain of the King's Guard for the true King! Long live Simon the Dragon! Long live Simon—my King!"

"Your words are food for my soul, Captain Blankenship."

"Yet not nearly as filling as horse-flesh, your Grace."

"Captain?" Simon said.

"Yes, my King."

"You have spoken long enough."

"Very well, then. Should we fall, my King, may the minstrels sing songs that tell our story for a hundred generations."

"We should go now, or the minstrels may begin

singing sooner than we would like."

Boone climbed on Simon's back and they took to the skies. Simon changed direction twice, in case they were followed. He felt strong from the meat in his belly, so he took a long route to their destination. He flew low over the sea for several minutes.

Simon felt movement on his back. He heard a scream. Boone had lost his grip. Boone fell and plunged deep into the dark water but rose quickly, crying out for help. Simon plucked him from the water and carried him to shore.

Simon stood aside. Boone shivered on his hands and knees. He coughed, over and over again. And then, he began to cry. Simon kept his distance and said nothing. He felt bad for his friend, who was finally experiencing the grief of his loss.

And then, Simon realized that Boone was not crying at all.

He was laughing.

"Have you gone mad?" Simon asked.

"I fell asleep!" Boone rolled over on his back.

"I fell asleep and nearly drowned! Promise me you'll not tell the minstrels this part of our story."

"You are mad," Simon said.

"Only my second dragon-ride, ever—and I've almost died. Being Captain of your Guard is proving to be most difficult."

Boone stood. He rubbed his arms and his teeth chattered.

"How much farther do we have to go?"

"Not far," Simon said.

Simon spread his wings, pushed off, and flew straight up.

Simon flew to the treetops and sliced branches with his talons.

Boone stared into the sky.

"What are you doi—?"

He jumped as tree branches rained to the ground.

Simon landed. He pushed the branches into a pile and set them ablaze with a quick bark of fire.

"Well," Boone said, "that skill has been of value today."

Minutes later, Boone was dry and warm. They took off again.

Simon landed in a clearing. He and Boone pushed their way through the heavy brush to reach the cave. Both of them were exhausted. Boone collapsed into a pile of straw grass. Simon lay down on the floor and closed his eyes. He felt a sharp pain inside his mouth. He sat up and worked his tongue between his back teeth. Something fell from his mouth and landed at his feet.

A bone.

Simon kicked the bone away in disgust. He looked over at Boone, who slept curled up on the grass. The scene reminded Simon of the first time he had seen Boone that way—ten years before. He sat and listened to Boone's steady breathing. Simon's thoughts wandered— back to the day he narrowly escaped death.

And the day he met his friend.

It was a bitter winter in Simon's eighth year. The snows were heavy and there were very few hunting parties. For four straight months, Simon remained in the same cave. During each of his four days as a human boy, he did nothing but burrow into piles of dead leaves and shiver—and wonder if each day would be his last.

At eight years of age, Simon was not an accomplished hunter—even as a dragon. That winter, he continually failed to catch up with anything of substance. In the quiet of winter, and under a blanket of snow, the animals seemed to sense the dragon. On the best days, Simon made due with a few thin rabbits. More often, he settled for mice or crows. Weakness grew as his body fed upon itself.

Simon the dragon lay at the mouth of his cave, listening to the wind whistle through the trees. He longed to hear anything else, even the night cries of the wolves, but even the wolves were silent. Perhaps they slept in their cozy dens—fat and happy after dining on a meal that would not keep a dragon alive for a single day.
Simon floated in and out of consciousness. In his moments awake, he believed he heard voices in the wind.

Die, the voices said.
Die. You were born to die. You were cursed to die. There is no being on earth that values your life. Your

death—will be the cause of celebration.

Die, Simon of Morgenwraithe.

Close your eyes—

and die.

Simon tensed in response to these voices, or thoughts, or whatever they were. He tried to raise his head. He wanted desperately to stand. He knew that he could no longer fly. Simon had not been able to produce fire for days. His belly cramped and sent fiery pains through him that made him scream.

It was midday.

And he was going to die. He closed his eyes—and he waited.

Behind his eyelids, Simon relaxed. He believed he had passed into the afterlife—a place of abundance and hope—where he would have another chance. He smelled the aroma of delicious meat—a welcoming feast.

A feast fit for a...

Simon sniffed. He opened one eye. His vision swam, but he could swear that he saw—

A young boy. A boy only a little older than he was.

And that boy carried a small deer. The deer was dead—with an arrow through its neck. The boy took a step toward Simon. And another step. He laid the deer in front of the dragon's mouth and backed away.

Simon stretched his neck and moved his jaws, but he was weak. So weak.

The boy took out a knife. He cut a piece of meat and held it above Simon's mouth. The dragon opened its jaws, and the boy dropped the meat inside.

The dragon exhaled without moving its jaws. Tiny puffs of smoke blew from his nostrils. The boy cut the heart from the deer. He held it above Simon's mouth and squeezed.

Simon swallowed. Moments later he chewed.

He chewed, and he chewed, and he chewed.

The boy fed the dragon until the deer was gone. And then, the dragon slept.

When he woke, the boy was still there. He was sleeping, too.

Simon felt something against his body. He looked down and then he looked at the boy.

The boy had covered him with his coat.

The boy had bruises on his arms and his neck. He had cuts around his eyes, and beneath them his face had patches of black and blue.

Simon tried to sit up. His talons scraped against the cave floor. The boy opened his eyes.

The boy and the dragon stared at each other.

"Thank you," Simon said.

The boy screamed. He pushed himself backward until his back hit the wall.

"No! No! You can't talk!"

"Of course, I can," Simon said. "I can talk much better than I can hunt."

"You're him, aren't you? The son of Bailin?"

"Do you know my father?" Simon asked.

The boy shook his head.

"Do you not...do you not know what became of the King?"

The boy lowered his voice.

"And...to the Queen?"

"They are dead," Simon said.

"I'm sorry," the boy said.

"What is your name?" Simon asked.

"Boone. Boone Blankenship."

"You saved my life."

"I could teach you how to hunt," Boone said. "It is the one thing that my father taught me to do. I do the hunting, so he can keep drinking."

"What happened to your face—and your arms?" Simon asked.

Boone stared at the floor.

"He gets mean when he's drunk. And he gets really mean when I don't bring home meat before dark."

"It is already dark," Simon said. "And I ate your deer."

"I'm not going home—I might not ever go home."

"How old are you?" Simon asked.

"Eleven."

"Do you have brothers or sisters?"

"I have an older brother—but he left."

"Where did he go?"

"I don't know. He left once and came back. But then he left again. Papa beat him pretty bad one night.

After Papa passed out, my brother left and never came back."

Simon picked up Boone's ragged coat and held it out.

"I am much better, now. You will need this."

Boone put on the coat.

"Why did you come here?" Simon asked. "Are you such a fierce hunter you have no fear of dragons?"

"I spend a lot of time in these woods. I've seen you—but I've yet to see any fire. I thought you might be sick. You looked hungry."

"I was starving."

"I will try to bag another deer after sunrise," Boone said. "And then, I have to get back."

"Why are you helping me?" Simon asked.

Boone stared at the floor and shuffled his feet.

"You were just a little kid. How old are you?"

"Eight," Simon said.

"I don't think a little kid could do anything bad enough to deserve what happened to you," Boone said.

"I could say the same for you, friend," Simon said. "Do you—do you love your father?"

"I love my mother," Boone said. "And that is all that matters."

A wolf howl brought Simon's thoughts back to the present. Boone rolled over and began snoring again.

I have only two friends in the world, Simon thought. The other one, I will likely never see again.

Simon crept to the corner of the cave. He picked up an old blanket and shook it to rid it of leaves and dust. He pulled it over Boone the best he could.

"Thank you," Boone mumbled in his sleep. He pulled the blanket up to his neck and curled up like a baby.

FIFTEEN

FIVE YEARS EARLIER

Word came to Castle Morgenwraithe that the eldest son of Viceroy Nicolas Lamont would be wed on the grounds of Castle Islemar. The Village of Islemar was a seaport, vital to the trade and defense of the entire kingdom. Merchant's vessels sailed in and out of its harbors every day.

Islemar was home to Lord Lamont, who had sworn his loyalty to three generations of Morgenwraithe Kings.

Lamont was named steward of Islemar and Viceroy of the kingdom by King Vonedor, Bailin's father. Lamont was a young man, at the time, and very popular among the people during difficult times. Vonedor looked to strengthen his place in the people's eyes by making a King's Decree that in the absence of a Morgenwraithe heir, the rule of the Kingdom would pass to Lamont and his heirs. The Kingdom drew much of its wealth from the merchant ship traffic at Islemar.

King Vonedor had two sons at the time of his decree. His first-born and heir, Bailin, was a strong and

spirited boy. Vonedor had no fear that there would ever
be a break in his bloodline.

Jaclyn Lamont smiled at the ladies, and at the shy
young boy who hid behind them. Jaclyn held her father's
hand. She looked up at him and smiled. Lord Lamont did
not look pleased at all.

"Lord Lamont," a lady dipped her head.

"Good day," Lamont said. "Begging your pardon,
but I was expecting Lord Sterling to be present at our
introductions."

"Begging your pardon, Viceroy," the woman
dipped her head even lower. "Lord Sterling developed
quite a thirst on our long journey—he will join us very
soon."

The boy continued to hide behind one of the
nursemaids. He sucked on his thumb.

"Very well," Lamont said. "What is your name,
madam?"

"I am Helga, Governess to the young King, my
Lord."

"May I present my daughter, Jaclyn," Lamont
said.

The Governess dipped her head once again.

"It is a great honor, My Lady," she said. "And
may I present, His Grace, King Lucien of
Morgenwraithe."

"What in the name of Vehallion's ghost are you
doing, Wench!"

Lord Sterling stomped across the floor, followed by a dozen members of the King's Guard. They all carried large mugs of ale. Sterling threw his at the nursemaid behind the Governess.

"Out of my way!" he pushed the Governess aside.

"First Knight of the Guard!" Sterling called out.

A Knight stepped to his side.

"Yes, My Lord."

"Get these women out of my sight," Lord Sterling said quietly.

"Yes, M—"

"And see that I never lay eyes upon them again," Lord Sterling said into the knight's ear. The knight nodded.

The King's Guard took the three women by the arm and pulled them from the room.

Sterling knelt before Lucien. He yanked the boy's thumb from his mouth. He spoke quietly into the boy's ear.

"You have shamed me and you have shamed the Kingdom, Your Grace," Sterling whispered without a hint of emotion.

"You will, from this day forward, act like a King, and not a frightened little girl. Or, I swear on my brother Bailin's grave, I will cut out your tongue and shove it down your throat until you are dead. Do I make myself clear, Your Grace?"

The terrified ten-year-old boy nodded. His wide eyes brimmed with tears.

Lord Sterling stood and clicked his heels together.

"King Lucien, of Morgenwraithe—may I present the Lady Jaclyn Lamont, who by decree and good faith, and unity of purpose—shall become thy bride and Queen of the Sovereign Kingdom of Morgenwraithe upon the King's thirteenth name day. Long live Queen Jaclyn!"

The King's Guard clicked their heels and raised their swords. Lord Lamont and his attendants did the same.

They all looked to Lucien and repeated along with him—

"Long live Queen Jaclyn!"

Lucien was embarrassed and frightened by the realization that he had humiliated his uncle. Lucien knew Lord Sterling was loyal to the throne of Morgenwraithe. But Lucien also knew his uncle was vicious and cruel. Sterling had no fear and no conscience.

Lucien moved his hand to wipe the tears from his eyes, but when he saw the hateful stare of Lord Sterling, he dropped his hand to his side. Lucien shuffled his feet and looked at Jaclyn. She smiled sweetly at him.

A flurry of conflicting emotions swept through Lucien's mind. He wished that he and the pretty little girl could run outside and play. But he knew he would never have another day of play for the rest of his life.

His confusion led to frustration and anger. The poisoned blood of his fathers brought about a change in Lucien that day. His eyes narrowed and his face grew stern.

On this day, Lord Sterling let Lucien know exactly where he stood.

He may be the King, but he would bleed—and die—like any other man.

Lucien stared at the little girl who continued to smile sweetly at him.

He hated her for her smile. He hated her for being less miserable than he was.

Jaclyn was too young and too naive to realize she had become the target of the hatred and fear that Lucien had nowhere else to place.

Jaclyn was startled awake that night. She had fallen asleep in strange quarters; in a high tower of her family's castle. The lower levels of the castle were given over to the visiting King, and his family and Guard. Jaclyn walked to the door and down the short hallway. She peeked into the other room where her parents were sleeping. Her father snored loudly—the wedding party had lasted for many hours. Lord Sterling and the King's Guard emptied glass after glass of wine and ale until Jaclyn was certain they would all die.

She silently wished they would.

Jaclyn went back to her room. She was about to climb back into bed when she heard a sound outside the window. She froze and strained to listen. The tower room stood high over the courtyard. The window was open, and there should be nothing on the ledges in the dead of night.

Please, do not let it be crows, Jaclyn thought.

She had heard the rumors—the whispers—when
they thought she could not hear. Lord and Lady Lamont
sheltered their daughter from the realities that lay
outside of their peaceful village. But Jaclyn was forever
curious, and she knew there was more to life in the
Kingdom than she was told. She became adept at
eavesdropping on the conversations of the castle
servants, and the knights and guards.

She heard about the horrors of the crows.

Jaclyn could not believe her ears, the night she
overheard two knights talking about what they had
witnessed at Castle Morgenwraithe. Men who were
thought to be enemies of the crown had their heads taken
and mounted atop the castle walls—

For the crows.

Jaclyn huddled beneath a stairwell one evening.
She listened as one knight told another that when a crow
eats human flesh, it goes for the eyes first. Jaclyn covered
her mouth but she could not stifle her cries. The knights
were horrified that she had overheard them. They tried
to calm her, but she pushed them away and ran. She hid
under her bed. She cried herself to sleep that night.

And on a similar night, there was something
outside of Jaclyn's bedroom window—waiting.

The seldom-used upper room contained only the
bed and a wardrobe. A broom stood in one corner. Jaclyn

picked it up. She crept toward the window.

"Please, go away!" she whispered aloud. She stopped at the window's edge and raised the broom above her head. She peered around the edge of the window and found herself face-to-face—

with the dragon.

Jaclyn dropped the broom and screamed. She inhaled to scream a second time, but the sound caught in her throat when she heard the dragon speak.

"Please," it said.

Jaclyn stared. Her jaw worked up and down but emitted no sound.

"Forgive me," the dragon said. And then he pushed away from the ledge outside the window, spread his wings and disappeared into the night sky.

Lord and Lady Lamont ran into the room. Lord Lamont carried a torch in one hand and his sword in the other.

"Jaclyn!" he called out. "What is it, child?"

Jaclyn looked out the window and then turned to her father.

"I had a bad dream."

SIXTEEN

The next night, Jaclyn lay awake for an hour. The King and his court had returned to Morgenwraithe, and she was back in her familiar surroundings and her own bed. But she could not sleep.

Jaclyn slipped out of her bed and got dressed. She lit an oil lamp and turned it low as she made her way to the vacant tower.

Jaclyn climbed the steps to the room where she had slept after her brother's wedding. She turned up the lamp and sat it in front of the window that faced the sea. She sat and waited.

I am being foolish, she thought. What do I hope to find? A bloodthirsty beast that may burn me alive at will?

She had heard the tales. Everyone had. The dragon was the son of the murdered King—cursed by a sorceress on the orders of the boy's own mother. Jaclyn could not begin to imagine the depth of such an evil.

Yet, the dragon had spoken to her, kindly.

Politely.

And gently.

The dragon grew to become more of an animal

with each passing year, the stories told. It burns crops at harvest time because its anger knows no limits. Its hatred for every man, woman, and child, is the only emotion that fuels its desires.

The dragon had been hunted. It had been shot at. It had been struck by arrows from the bows of the most feared archers in the Kingdom—yet it lived to fly the night skies and terrorize villages far and wide.

Jaclyn had never heard it said that the dragon could speak.

What does that mean? she wondered.

If there have been no tales about the dragon who can speak, then perhaps some of the stories are untrue.

Or, she thought,

What if they are ALL untrue?

Movement caught Jaclyn's eye.

She jumped up and ran to the window.

There he was. Gliding, west to east. And then, east to west. Jaclyn doused the lamp. She stood in front of the window. She was not certain, but she guessed that the dragon was able to see her silhouette.

The dragon crossed the sky again, and then Jaclyn lost sight of him. Moments later she heard a noise— above her head. She heard another noise. This time, outside the window.

Jaclyn took a step toward the window. She leaned outside. She froze.

The dragon perched on a bastion.

Jaclyn looked into the dragon's eyes. They were only a few paces apart.

Jaclyn struggled to speak.

"I...I want to show you something."

She could hear the dragon's heavy breathing. She saw and smelled the smoke that spilled from around its enormous teeth.

Jaclyn reached into her gown and took out a piece of parchment. With trembling hands, she held the parchment in front of her as she leaned farther out of the window.

The dragon leaned forward. His eyes narrowed as he looked at the quivering page.

"Can...you...read?"

Jaclyn jumped when the dragon threw back his head. It loosed a laugh—along with a bolt of blue and orange flame.

Jaclyn could not move.

The dragon lowered its head.

"I'm sorry, I'm sorry," it said. "That happens, sometimes. I cannot always control it—especially when I am surprised."

"You can talk," Jaclyn whispered. "And you can read?"

"Please, tell no one," the dragon whispered. "I have a reputation to think about."

Jaclyn nodded. Her eyes were wide.

"That was a joke," the dragon said. "Perhaps, not a good one. My opportunities to have a conversation are so few and far between, as you might imagine."

"It's all lies," Jaclyn whispered. "The stories—they are all lies."

"Stories?" the dragon said. "Stories about me? I am certain there are more than a few."

"There are hundreds," Jaclyn said. "I have heard them my entire life."

"Some of them are true, of course," the dragon said. "Those that speak of my speed and agility—my ability to dodge arrows—"

"They say you cause the people of entire villages to starve by destroying their fields," Jaclyn said. "They say you have been known to pluck babies from their mother's breast."

"Lies!" the dragon barked.

"They say you lurk in the shadows and steal meat from hunters."

"That one is true. It gives me no pleasure, but I must eat. Or I will die."

"Shall I call you 'Simon'?" Jaclyn asked.

"That is my name."

"Why were you outside of this window—on the night of my brother's wedding?" Jaclyn asked.

"I hoped to see my brother," Simon said. "To catch even a glimpse…would mean something. I cannot risk going near the village or the castle."

"How did you know he would be here?" Jaclyn

asked.

"I have friends," Simon said.

Jaclyn looked sad.

"I have to go," she said. "You need not lie to me. Please…be careful."

She turned away.

"Wait!" Simon said.

Jaclyn faced him.

"I have…only one friend. He told me Lucien would be here."

"What else did he tell you?"

"That you are to marry the King."

"Your brother has returned to Morgenwraithe. Yet, here you are."

Simon stared out to sea and said nothing.

"What is your friend's name?" Jaclyn asked.

"You will marry my brother, and you will be my Queen. My brother rules a Kingdom that offers a fortune to the man who slays me."

Simon turned and stared into Jaclyn's eyes.

"You will soon be Queen of the Realm that holds a bounty on my head. The time may come when I lie bleeding and pierced by a thousand arrows—but I will never surrender my friend."

In the light of the moon, Simon saw a tear stream down Jaclyn's cheek.

"Why do you cry?" Simon asked.

"We are told that your heart beats only for

vengeance," she said. "It is said that your curse was the judgment of the gods for the sins of your family. Yet, in truth, you are far nobler than anyone I have ever known."

"What kind of Kingdom is this," Simon said. "Where simple loyalty to one's friend is uncommon?"

"A hard and cold place," Jaclyn said. "My father says Lord Sterling fills your brother's head with wickedness."

Jaclyn continued in a whisper.

"I am forbidden to speak of such things."

"As well you should be," Simon said. "Lord Sterling will not abide a voice of dissension—even from the Queen of the Realm."

"How will I survive?" Jaclyn cried. "Inside the castle all day and every day—with that foul man?"

Jaclyn sighed.

"I so wish this curse could be broken and you could take the throne that should have been yours."

Simon rose and spread his wings.

"Do you see? The curse holds power far beyond my body. You must guard your words, my future Queen. In the world you enter, the very walls have eyes and ears. You must remember this, at all times."

"You sound just like my father," Jaclyn said.

"Both of us want you to live," Simon said.

He raised his head. Flame burst from his nostrils.

"Can you…will you come back?" Jaclyn asked.

"You should not ask such a thing. I can bring you

nothing but trouble."

"I could be...I could be your friend, too." Jaclyn said.

Simon laughed. Smoke rolled from his mouth.

"The King's Guard will be at your beck and call, night and day. You will have servants and nursemaids. And thousands of adoring subjects."

"Yes," Jaclyn said. "And the same number of friends I have now. Zero."

"I beg to differ, My Lady," Simon said.

"You have one."

The dragon leaped into the night and disappeared over the sea.

SEVENTEEN

Jaclyn's mother jostled her awake an hour after daybreak.

"Gracious, child!" Lady Lamont said. "Do you intend to sleep the entire day away? Come, now. Up! Up! There is much for you to learn before you take your place beside the King!"

"I have plenty of time to learn to be a Lady, Mother," Jaclyn said. "I am not an imbecile."

"Not an imbecile!" Lady Lamont said.

She grabbed Jaclyn's hand.

"One broken—no, two broken nails—and mud beneath them all!" she cried.

"My daughter—destined to rule these lands— spends her days running after the sons of commoners!"

"We have fun, Mother."

"Fun? Fun does not prepare a lady to rule the people! Fun does not prepare a Queen to represent her Kingdom with elegance and grace!"

"But fun will let you pull a fat frog from the mud down at the stream."

"Well, there you have it, then!" Lady Lamont

threw up her hands.

"After your wedding, you and King Lucien can lead us all down to the stream for our very first Royal 'Frog-Pulling'!"

"Yes, Mother. That would be so much less dignified that everyone getting drunk and dancing until they fall down."

"Perhaps, one day, a Queen with years of rule behind her might bring about a change in tradition," Lady Lamont said. "But those days are far, far away. Get up! Your bath has been drawn and you have a new dress to try on."

Jaclyn groaned and got out of bed. She bathed, and a maid washed her hair. Another maid came in and helped Jaclyn into her new dress.

One of the maids cinched up her corset.

"Ow!" Jaclyn yelled.

"What does it matter how I look, if I cannot breathe?"

"There is no beauty without pain," one maid said.

"It is the way of women."

"I will be changing that, when I am Queen," Jaclyn said.

"You may as well complain about men-folk liking to get drunk and root around like swine," the other maid giggled.

Jaclyn was escorted to the parlor, where she met with two older ladies. Those ladies were also squeezed into their tiny-waisted dresses, but they did not seem to mind at all.

"Jaclyn," one of them said. "Today, we will teach you to walk."

"To walk?" Jaclyn said. "You cannot be serious!"

"Your dress, your face, and your walk will be the first impression you give as the Royal Representative of the Kingdom, my child," the first lady said.

"You cannot overestimate the importance of your walk," the second lady said. "Your face, is a given. You are an exquisite beauty, child—just like your mother!"

"Your wardrobe is also a given," the first lady said. "The finest seamsters in the land will provide you with the finest dresses. This leaves your walk—which we will begin to perfect today."

"Jaclyn," the first lady continued. "Walk across the floor for us. Pretend that you are meeting the prince of a neighboring Kingdom."

Jaclyn walked across the parlor floor. She stopped and turned.

"I can hardly believe my eyes!" the first lady said.

"Unlike anything I have ever seen!" the second lady said.

"Jaclyn, have you ever toiled on a farm?" the first lady asked.

"I beg your pardon?" Jaclyn asked.

"Have you ever handled a plow—behind an ox or a mule?" he second lady asked. "Because that is precisely the way you walk!"

The day was long and Jaclyn hated every minute of it.

She yawned as she got ready for bed. She filled her oil lamp and left it beside her door; prepared to make her way to the tower again. She lay down and closed her eyes. She opened them moments later, horrified that she had fallen asleep so quickly.

Jaclyn peeked out of her door. Light shone beneath her parents' door. She dared not lie down again. She sat on the floor beside her door and thought of questions to ask of her mysterious new friend.

Jaclyn woke with a start. The first rays of dawn struck her face. She was furious with herself.

That day was more of the same; the two ladies training her in the ways befitting the Queen of the Kingdom of Morgenwraithe. Walking, bowing, waving, and mastering the graceful form of the proper curtsy filled the day's agenda.

Jaclyn's taskmasters finally seemed to believe that she might be transformed into a proper lady after all.

Jaclyn prepared to sneak out of her room and visit the tower again that night. She peered out of her doorway until she saw the space beneath her parents' door go dark. She waited, but she remained standing. She refused to let sleep overcome her again. Jaclyn had no way of knowing if Simon was still nearby.

Jaclyn stayed in the shadows on her journey, avoiding the guard towers. She tripped once and fell, spilling some of her lamp's oil. She waited in the dark.

The noise had not alerted anyone of her presence.

Jaclyn lit the lamp and placed it in a tower window. She squinted at the night sky. There was very little moonlight.

There were three windows that faced out to the sea. Jaclyn walked between them, pausing to look out of each one. She grew tired. With each passing minute, she became more depressed. She sat down on the window seat.

"I missed you last night."

Jaclyn shrieked and nearly fell to the floor. She cried out again when she twisted her ankle. She scraped her left elbow against the rough stone of the window ledge.

Jaclyn gathered herself and leaned out of the window. The dragon perched on the bastion—his usual place.

"How long have you been there?" Jaclyn asked. "I did not see or hear you!"

"If I moved about like a flying ox, I would have been dead before now. Perhaps that is one reason why so few dragons remain."

"That is not the reason, Mr. Dragon," Jaclyn said.

"My name is not Mr. Dragon. It's Simon."

"Tearing people in half with their talons, biting off their heads, burning houses and crops and livestock—this is why there are no more dragons."

"I'm not like that," Simon said.

"That is part of the curse, is it not?" Jaclyn said. "You are feared and hated and hunted down, regardless of what lives in your heart."

"Yes," Simon said. "You must admit, it is the perfect curse. Such great power and strength—yet bound to a life of loneliness—feared and hunted by everyone.

"Even one's own brother."

"We do not have to speak of such things here," Jaclyn said. "Here, in this place, you are safe. Here, we can be friends."

"Friends," Simon said softly. He looked out to the sea. He exhaled and dark smoke rolled from his mouth.

"Soon, you will become Queen, and move to Morgenwraithe. You will live in the place where my name will be vilified until the day that someone claims my life."

"Perhaps I can reason with the King," Jaclyn said. "If you would just remain hidden for a while, I could tell him that—"

A blast of flame shot from Simon's nostrils. He whipped his head around to face Jaclyn.

"I do little but hide from huntsmen every day of my existence! I am bound by the endless sea on three sides of the Kingdom. The fourth side leads only to the poorest lands where thousands see me as the answer to their hunger. My sanctuaries are discovered as quickly as I find them."

Jaclyn said nothing for a few moments.

"I have heard a tale—a tale that is difficult to

believe."

"What tale?" Simon asked.

"There are some who say that you change—you change back into a boy. For a short time."

Simon said nothing.

"Is it true?" Jaclyn whispered.

"It would make no difference if it were true," Simon said.

"I think it would give you hope. Hope, that one day, the curse could be broken."

"And I think such a thing would serve only to torture me—with what will never be."

Jaclyn began to cry.

"Being your friend is the hardest thing I have ever done."

Simon spread his wings.

"It is certainly not the wisest—"

The door burst open. The shouts of men filled the room. Torches and arrows flew.

Jaclyn's father grabbed her arms. She screamed a warning to Simon and then watched in horror as fiery arrows flew at him from the bows of the castle guards.

Most of the arrows bounced away from the dragon's scales, but Jaclyn saw two flaming arrows pierce Simon's right wing as he pushed into the sky. Another flaming arrow pierced his left wing.

Jaclyn struggled against her father's grip. She got away and ran to the window. She watched as Simon flew out to sea. Tears streamed down Jaclyn's cheeks as she saw the oil-soaked arrows spread flames across the span of the dragon's wings. She watched him plummet down—down, until she could see no more.

The great dragon plunged headlong either into the sea—
Or onto the rocky earth.

EIGHTEEN

Five Years Later

Jaclyn and her handmaid, Helena, entered the Grand Hall. King Lucien was attended by five seamsters: two men and three women. They hovered around the King like bees, fitting him for his new robes in anticipation of the King's name day celebration. The ceremony and festival would celebrate his fifteenth year.

"Oh, look, Helena!" Jaclyn clapped her hands together.

"How magnificent you look, Your Grace!"

Jaclyn's good mood faded instantly. She had not seen a bored Lord Sterling leaning against the wall behind the velvet drapes.

"Yes, the King looks simply marvelous," Sterling said. "And I see that the Queen's belly is still flat. Not the result we had foreseen when we planned for the future of Morgenwraithe—and its throne."

Helena rushed off to assist one of the seamstresses.

Jaclyn blushed at Lord Sterling's remarks. She offered her help to the seamstresses, but they were terrified by the thought of engaging the Queen in such a menial task.

Sterling cleared his throat and pushed himself away from the wall. He stumbled, spilling wine from a priceless chalice that bore the shield and banners of the Kingdom of Morgenwraithe.

"Perhaps these times call for the Queen to spend less time walking the gardens with her handmaid," Sterling said. He pointed at Lucien with his cup.

"And as for His Majesty, perhaps less time off hunting with the King's Guard. And less time shooting arrows into straw men—and straw dragons!"

"Ow!" a seamstress cried out. She had stuck her finger with a needle.

The castle's servants were terrified in Sterling's presence. He held every one of them in contempt and seemed to feed off of their fears. Sterling doled out punishment for the slightest mistakes. The seamstress had just made one.

"Come here," Sterling scowled. The girl stood before him, whimpering.

"Did you not hear me speaking?" Sterling asked.
"Yes, My Lord."
The girl's blood dripped on the floor.
"I'm so sorry, My Lord."

"Dear Uncle," Lucien said. "I should very much like to be finished with this ordeal. Please, allow the girl to continue her duties."

"So, you're in a hurry, eh, Your Grace?" Sterling slurred. "Can't wait to get back to your bow and your scary dragons—"

"How else shall I prepare to face the real dragon?" Lucien asked. "He dared to show himself in the village—he killed two of my Guards!"

Sterling turned up his chalice and emptied it.

"I will add fifty to the Guard! We should have had that beast's head long ago! Perhaps, putting a few Royal Knight's heads on the wall will convince the others that their failures are unacceptable!"

"I want to slay the dragon, myself," Lucien said.

Sterling waved his hand in the air.

"Of course, you do! A childish dream for a childish King!"

The servants were afraid to breathe. Or to move. They stared at the floor.

Sterling placed his hand under the chin of the seamstress. He raised her head.

"See to the King's dress—so he may hurry back to his playthings!"

"Yes, My L—"

Sterling slapped the girl with his open hand, knocking her to the floor.

He glared at Lucien, spun around, and left the room.

NINETEEN

The young man sat in the chair, rocking slowly as he held his baby daughter. She was a delightful child who almost never cried. She had never been fussy at all until lately. Her little tummy did not care for goat's milk.

The man's wife lay on a bed in the corner. His mother-in-law sniffed as she held the barely conscience young lady's hand and wiped sweat from her forehead with a cool cloth.

The man looked up at the open door. His father-in-law stood there, facing the open field.

The baby tottered against her father's chest and went to sleep. The man laid the baby down on blankets piled in the corner of the tiny house and stepped outside.

"Without medicine, she will die," the man said.

His father-in-law stared blankly—at nothing.

"She is not the first, Benjamin. And not likely the last."

"And we are to accept this?" Benjamin said. "We should have medicine! We have a treaty with Morgenwraithe to receive goods from the merchant ships, and we receive nothing! Why do we tolerate—?"

"The treaty has known five generations. Do you

think to represent all of the Southland?"

"If no one else will, then why not?" Benjamin said. "We keep our end of the treaty. We stay south of the Kingdom's borders. We do not interfere with the King's business. We receive nothing for most of a year, and our people grow sick and die!"

"Lord Sterling has explained—"

"He lies!" Benjamin said. "There has been little honor in Morgenwraithe for years. And under Sterling, it has none at all."

"What would you have us do? Gather the men to war? March on the border and meet the King's Guard and army in combat? We would die like dogs and leave our women and children to be—"

"There is support for a rebellion in the north," Benjamin said. "Surely you have not forgotten those men—"

"Forgotten? Ha! I wager you have forgotten what became of those men! Their heads line the top of the castle wall!"

Benjamin's mother-in-law ran through the door. She fell into her husband's arms, weeping.

Benjamin and the older man stared at one another as the woman wailed.

Her energy spent, the woman pushed herself away from her husband. She put her arms around Benjamin and buried her face in his chest.

"No, no, no, no!" came her muffled sobs.

The baby cried.

The woman patted Benjamin's chest and dried her eyes.

"I will see to her, Ben."

Ben nodded.

"I am going to speak to the men," Ben said to his father-in-law. "Something must be done."

The older man scowled.

"I grieve with you, Ben. She was my daughter. But do not allow grief to make you foolish. You are not the only one to lose a wife, or a child. The Council will—"

"The Council does noth—" Ben remembered that his mother-in-law and his daughter could hear him.

"The Council has done nothing. They have not even crossed the border to make an inquiry."

"I trust the Kingdom no more than you, Ben. But you must be careful what you say. If you had been born here, perhaps the Council would hear you. You gained a measure of trust when you wed my daughter, but that trust is not absolute. You must think of what is best for the baby."

"I am thinking about her. I am thinking that I cannot bear to watch her become ill and die."

"Ben...,"

The older man watched his son-in-law's back as he stormed off toward the village square. He shook his head.

"May the gods be with us."

Ben found a group of men gathered in the village square in front of the row of shops. He told them of the death of his wife. More people gathered to listen.

"I know I am not one of you. You have accepted me, and for that I am grateful. But our people are ill. Sickness is among us, and this is not a new thing. But we know there are medicines that reach the Kingdom at the ports of Islemar.

"We have a valid treaty with Morgenwraithe — which they choose to ignore.

"Our people are dying. They are dying, and we are doing nothing to stop it. Is this not the purpose of your Counsel?"

The people were silent. Some of them turned and walked away.

"Does no one care?" Ben shouted at their backs.

"What would you have us do?" one old man asked. "March on Morgenwraithe?"

"March to war?" Ben said. "No. But to at least march into the village and question the crown and its decision to ignore the treaty made by its own King!"

"We would be slaughtered at the border!" cried one man.

"Will this be your answer when death comes to your door?" Ben asked. "Will this be your answer when it is your wife or your child — ?"

The man balled his hands into fists.

"You shut your mouth, and you shut it now, boy! We took you in as one of our own, and you propose to stand in our midst and tell us what to do?"

The man turned and looked at the others.

"I propose that the Council banishes this man from our village—before he brings the wrath of Morgenwraithe down upon our heads!"

The people murmured.

"And I tell you," Ben said, "that I will stand on this very spot at noon tomorrow. I will march to the border, and into Morgenwraithe. I will march with those who also seek what is just and fair—or I will go alone. As for the remainder of this day—"

Ben glared at the man and focused his anger.

"I must return home and bury my wife."

TWENTY

Ben walked into the village at just before noon. He had passed no one by the time he reached the market. He rounded a corner and saw a woman with two young children. The woman gathered her children and they rushed inside the door of a shop.

The door slammed shut.

The weather was pleasant, yet the shops' doors and windows were closed.

Two more doors slammed shut along the main street of the market.

Ben's spirits fell when he saw that there were only two boys in the square. He looked up at the sun. It was directly overhead.

"Is it time for us to go?" a boy asked.

"All of two brave souls," Ben said.

"There are more of us—but not many," another boy said. "They told us to fetch them if you showed up."

"What do you mean by that?" Ben asked. "Is our cause not just? Are we wrong to expect the terms of our treaty to be met?"

"Aye, the cause is just," the boy said. "There are

eleven of us. But only two as old as you. We've all lost family to illness."

Ben looked around.

"Where are these others? In hiding?"

"We thought it best to wait for you. Some of the merchants had unkind words for us. Some of them made threats against us."

"Threats?" Ben said. "For daring to stand up for the lives of our people?"

"You heard them yesterday. They are afraid that the Kingdom will sense a threat and send their armies across the border."

"That would be madness," Ben said. "Attempting to cross the canyon would cost them many lives."

"How many do they have to spare?" one boy asked. "And who can know what weapons they may have gathered from across the seas? If our people continue to fall to sickness and disease, Morgenwraithe will learn of it. This may even be their cruel intent! We should wait no longer."

"Shall we fetch the others?" the other boy asked.

"No," Ben said. "We will go to them. Our enemies lie to the north. Not in this village."

They met up with the others at the northern end of the village.

Their group numbered twelve.

"We will travel until sundown," Ben said. "A full day's march tomorrow will bring us to the border in time to rest before nightfall. We will cross the border under cover of darkness.

The afternoon of the second day, they crossed a rushing river and entered the mouth of the canyon that led to the border of the Kingdom of Morgenwraithe.

One hour later, Ben stopped them.

"There is a spring ahead, near the mouth of the canyon. It brings forth the purest water. We will drink our fill and replenish our skins. And we will wait there for nightfall."

When the spring was in sight, Ben went to it and drank. The other men followed him.

"What is this?" one of the young boys said. "Abandoned treasure?"

A large trunk stood against the wall of the canyon on the opposite side from the spring. Four of the boys ran toward the chest.

The boy in the lead stumbled when his ankle hit a vine.

A sharpened stake swung from behind the trunk and impaled the boy's face.

"No!" Ben jumped up and yelled at the other boys, but they could not move fast enough.

Three more concealed triggers launched sharpened stakes from behind the trunk in powerful arcs.

One boy was hit in the neck, another in the chest. They died instantly.

The last boy was hit in the stomach.

Ben ran toward the boy who was still alive, but he stopped when he saw the way strewn with more vines.

The boy's eyes met Ben's. His jaw worked while blood spilled from the corners of his mouth.

"Tell my mother—"

Those were his last words.

Three arrows flew past Ben's head. He whipped around and looked toward the mouth of the canyon. The entire opening was filled with shields, helmets, and bows. Ben dropped to the ground as another flurry of arrows flew past him.

"Get down!" he screamed.

Three more of their number fell to arrows.

"Retreat! Retreat!" Ben screamed. "Stay low and run!"

Ben ran, not knowing if any were left alive to follow him. He looked over his shoulder when he reached the river.

He saw one boy, running for his life.

"This way!" Ben yelled.

He turned to the west and ran along the river's edge. He looked once to see if the boy was still following him. He was.

Ben found what he had been waiting for—deep water.

He plunged in and swam downstream.

I pray that you can swim, he thought.

When his shoulder ached so badly that he could hardly stand it, Ben swam to the river's edge and climbed onto dry land.

The boy followed him.

They huddled behind a fallen tree and stared upstream for an hour. The shadows grew long. No one came.

Ben stood and stretched. He stepped away and relieved himself. When he returned, the boy sat with his elbows on his knees. His hands covered his face as he wept.

Ben put a hand on the boy's shoulder. The boy jumped. He wiped his eyes.

"They haven't followed us," Ben said. "It will be nightfall soon."

The boy nodded.

"I am sorry. I will try to behave like a man, my Lord."

"I am no Lord," Ben said. "And even if I was, we have seen war together. What is your name?"

"Liam."

"I believe we will be safe here tonight, Liam. We will get an early start and make it back to the village by nightfall tomorrow."

"Yes, my Lord,"

Ben started to object, but thought better of it. He rolled his left shoulder several times and then dug his fingers in to massage the muscle. The shoulder had pained him for thirteen years—after his arm was wrenched out of its socket. It had never healed to where it did not ache.

"How old are you?" Ben asked.

"Sixteen, my Lord."

"You knew the other boys, didn't you?"

Liam nodded.

"One of them was my brother. He wants us to…he wanted me to tell our mother that he loved her."

"We have cheated death today, Liam. I can say that about only one other man on this earth—and he is my flesh and blood. I would never have him refer to me as a superior. And I will not ask more of you. My name is Benjamin."

Liam shook his head.

"I…I do not think that I can. I would forever see my father's face, and he would feel shame."

"I will explain it to him—"

"He died," Liam said, "seven months ago—of the same fever. If he knew that I failed to show respect to a man of authority, he would feel that I showed him disrespect, as well."

"Very well," Ben said. "I will not ask you to go against your father's wishes."

"Thank you, Lord Blankenship."

TWENTY-ONE

The Captain of the Border Guard ordered his officers to stay with him in the mouth of the canyon.

The air was thick with the smell of blood and vomit. The border guard was staffed by young men who had never seen conflict, let alone the kind of damage that their spear traps were capable of.

"Remove these men from the traps," the Captain ordered.

"Men?" the first officer said. "These are boys!"

"I do not care if they were nursemaids!" the Captain roared. "We are charged with the defense of the border, and the border came under assault!"

"They carried no weapons," another officer said.

The Captain stepped in front of that man and grabbed him by the collar.

"Is that what you wish to tell Raynard? Or Lord Sterling? That their Border Guard murdered an invading force of unarmed children?"

"No, Captain."

"What do we tell them?" the first officer asked.

The Captain paced and stroked his chin.

"When is the celebration—for the King's name day?" he asked.

"In two days, Captain," the first officer answered.

"Ah!" the Captain winced. "Sterling will be in a particularly foul mood. This will not bode well for us."

The Captain stepped next to a dead man with an arrow through his heart. He raised his boot and kicked the man in the side.

"They will not send us more men," he said. "But they will demand even more of us. More patrols. More men on night watch. And more reports sent to the castle."

The Captain stared each of his officers in the eye.

"Clear the bodies. We will reset the traps when the blood is dry, and the stench is gone.

"This day—did not happen. Make this clear to your men. If I learn that a single word of these events has passed beyond our ranks, I will find the loose tongue and cut it out. And then I will have that man's head! Do I make myself clear?"

"Yes, Captain!" the officers said in unison.

"What do we do with them?" the first officer asked.

The Captain started toward the mouth of the canyon.

"Burn the bodies."

TWENTY-TWO

Simon and Boone stood high on top of the hill. A broken-down stone wall was all that was left of an ancient outpost. The outpost had not been used for generations—since the reign of Simon's great-grandfather. There had been no one foolish enough to challenge the might and power of the Morgenwraithe family since that time.

Simon looked down on the Royal tournament arena, which was decorated with brightly colored tents and banners. Boone held his new spyglass to his eye.

"This glass is amazing!" Boone said. "I have the vision of a dragon now!"

"How many stripes are there on the banner beneath the King' seat?" Simon asked. "And what is their color?"

"That's an easy one. Five red stripes."

"Maybe the glass will prove useful, after all," Simon said.

"Coming here is not the wisest thing you've ever done," Boone said.

"I will not do anything foolish," Simon said. "I'm

not about to fly down there and present the King with a gift for his name day. This wall shields us. We'll go no closer."

"On a day when every soldier in the realm is in full armor and carrying swords, shields, and full quivers, even being this close is madness," Boone said.

"Rest easy, Boone. Perhaps you might glimpse the queen's handmaiden again."

"Oh. Her," Boone said. "The girl who you said was the second loveliest you had ever seen! Who could possibly be more lovely—the Queen herself?"

Boone lowered the glass and stared at Simon.

"Say. Have you seen the Queen?"

Simon snorted.

"And what…what if I have? Many people have seen the Queen."

"Ho, ho, ho!" Boone laughed. "When did you see the Queen? And more importantly, has she seen you?"

"It was a very long time ago…"

Boone studied his friend's expression.

"I do not believe it. You have seen her. And you have feelings for her! Your brother's bride!"

Simon stared down. He worked his jaw, and a growl sounded in his throat.

"I am here to see the kind of celebration that should have been held in my name."

"So, we are risking our lives so you may shed a tear for what might have been," Boone said.

Simon snorted a blast of fire.

MY NAME IS SIMON 125

"We are here so that I do not forget what was stolen from me. This sight burns its place into my heart and my mind. I will regain my place at the head of this Kingdom—even if it comes down to my final breath."

Boone nodded and patted the dragon's side.

"Forget I said anything. I like the way your mind works, my king."

The people filed into the arena. The sounds of trumpets filled the air, signaling the entrance of the King and his court.

"I can't see them," Boone said. "They've shaded the Royal seating area from the sun. How much longer must we stay? I'm getting a bad feeling about this."

The trumpets sounded again.

"Let's go," Simon said. "It would be wise if we—"

"Wait," Boone said. "There is another procession coming up the road. What is that?"

"Oh, no," Simon said. He pulled Boone behind the wall.

"What is it?"

"No...it cannot be!"

TWENTY-THREE

Queen Jaclyn walked two paces behind King Lucien. Lord Sterling walked at the King's side. Sterling was suffering the effects of the previous night's wine and he was in a particularly foul mood. The Captain of the King's Guard, Raynard, walked next to Sterling. He joined Sterling in the earlier night of debauchery and also felt a degree of misery.

Raynard was Sterling's man, his loyalty secured with lands and coin and a common lust for power and dominance.

Helena walked with Jaclyn. When they reached the platform where the King's and Queen's seats were, Helena turned away. Jaclyn grabbed her hand.

"Please, stay with me."

Helena was afraid. Sterling turned and glared at them both.

"Begging your pardon, My Lord," Jaclyn said. "I am not feeling well."

Sterling grunted but turned his attention elsewhere. He snatched a mug of ale from a servant boy, turned it up, and drained it dry. He did the same to two more mugs.

The tournament announcer welcomed the people and introduced the Queen. Jaclyn stood and waved and smiled.

"We love you Queen Jaclyn!" a woman cried from the crowd. Jaclyn's smile broadened. She was a popular Queen and a favorite of the people.

Sterling ignored the crowd's display of affection.

The King was far less popular, suffering from what most knew or suspected—that the King was totally under Sterling's control. The applause for Lucien was long and loud, but without passion. Many of those who cheered kept a wary eye on Sterling. No one dared to stand accused of failing to show proper respect.

For the next thirty minutes, a procession of dancers, jesters, and jugglers performed before the Royal platform. Sterling grew drunk and impatient. He stood and yelled for the performers to stop.

He cleared his throat and belched.

"I have searched, far and wide, to find the perfect gift for my nephew's fifteenth name day. And I believe I have succeeded!"

The crowd roared its approval.

Sterling held his hand out toward Lucien.

"King Lucien, son of King Bailin, my beloved brother, please rise."

Lucien stood.

Sterling turned and stumbled, sloshing ale from his mug.

"Captain of the Guard!" Sterling said. "A

blindfold, if you please!"

The crowd murmured in anticipation as the King was blindfolded. Sterling led Lucien by the arm to the front edge of the Royal platform.

Members of the King's Guard stood before the arena gates. Sterling nodded, and the gates opened.

The crowd noise swelled. There were shrieks and screams. Sterling held fast to Lucien's arms.

Lucien struggled.

"Uncle, please! I want to see!"

Queen Jaclyn stood. She was unsteady on her feet. Helena leaped to her side.

"No," Jaclyn whispered.

Six strong men entered the arena, each holding the end of a heavy chain. At the end of the six chains—

Was a dragon.

Sterling let go of Lucien's arms. Lucien tore away the blindfold.

He stared at the spectacle before him in disbelief. And anger. And fear.

Lucien knew instantly that the dragon was not his brother. This dragon was obviously very old. It was not large as dragons go. Many of its scales were broken or missing, as were some of its teeth. The dragon was a ruddy, dull brown—drab and mottled.

The dragon's jaws were bound shut with a heavy leather muzzle. The muzzle was secured around the back of the dragon's head with more chains. The dragon thrashed its head back and forth. Only pathetic and weak mewing sounds escaped its clenched jaws.

"Where did you find this ugly beast?" Raynard asked Sterling.

"I purchased it from a band of nomad hunters from deep in the Southlands," Sterling said. "They sent a messenger, saying they had captured the cursed son of Bailin. I knew they were mistaken about that, but I was curious enough to go and look. They thought to ask a small fortune for this worn and weathered old beast, but common sense took hold. I let them know that favor in the Kingdom of Morgenwraithe is worth more than mere gold."

Sterling faced the crowd and chanted.
"Lucien!
"Lucien!
"Lucien!"
The crowd picked up the chant, and the roar shook the arena. Soon, other cries were heard above the fray.

"Slay the filthy beast!"
"Cut off its head!"
"Long live King Lucien—the dragonslayer!"
"Kill it! Kill it!"
"Rid our lands of these foul creatures!"

Lucien did not know what to do. He turned to Lord Sterling.

"Uncle, what am I to—?"

Sterling held out his hand to Raynard.

"Your sword, please, Sire!"

Raynard handed over his sword. Sterling offered it to Lucien.

"Let your legend become known this day—throughout the land!" Sterling shouted. "Slay a dragon!"

Sterling pointed at Queen Jaclyn.

"Slay a dragon and put a baby boy inside of your Queen, and your legacy is complete!"

Lucien stared at the sword.

"But, I—"

Sterling pumped his fist and chanted again.

"Lucien!

"Lucien!

"All hail the King—slayer of dragons!"

Jaclyn grabbed Lucien's arm.

"No, Lucien. You do not have to—"

Lucien jerked his arm away. His face was red and sweat appeared on his forehead. He trembled. The roar of the crowd swelled in waves. Lucien took the sword from Sterling's hand.

He faced the crowd and lifted the sword over his head.

The noise was deafening. People threw flowers into the air. They floated down and landed in front of the Royal platform.

Lucien waded through the flower petals. Raynard

and his second fell in beside the King. Sterling followed behind, scanning the crowd with his stare between gulps of ale. The foursome marched to the middle of the area — and in front of the dragon.

"Are you ready, your Grace?" Raynard asked.

Lucien gripped the sword with white-knuckled hands. He nodded.

Raynard nodded to two of the strong men. The men released their chains.

The dragon jerked his wings side-to-side. The four remaining men held on tightly. One of them lost his footing, and the dragon threw him into the air. The other two strong men chased down the loose chains. Some of the closest members of the arena audience deserted their seats.

The dragon had exhausted itself in its desperate move. Its body heaved as it struggled to breathe with its jaws clamped shut. The men regained their grips on the chains.

"The beast has a little fight left in him, after all!" Sterling laughed.

The crowd picked up the chant again.

"Lucien!

"Lucien!

"Lucien!"

"Loose the beast!" Lucien cried.

"What?" Raynard said. He stepped closer to Lucien's side.

"Please, your Grace. Let the beast spend more of its strength. It remains a danger—"

Sterling said nothing. He stared at Lucien with an amused smirk.

"What do you mean to do, Captain of the Guard?" Lucien growled. "Leave me nothing to do but climb on top of it while it is dying? Why not just have the queen kill it?"

"Please, Lord Sterling," Raynard pleaded. "Reason with—"

"Must I remind you, Captain," Sterling said. "Lucien is your King! And I believe he has given you an order."

Raynard turned slowly toward the dragon. The men holding the chains looked to Raynard for direction.

Lucien watched, and in that moment, the noise ceased to exist.

He turned and looked at his Uncle.

This is what he planned all along, Lucien thought.

And I have taken his bait, like a proud and ignorant animal. I will die, now—and my uncle may as well have driven his own blade into my heart.

Lucien looked toward the Royal platform. Jaclyn stood between her parents, crying. She clutched her father's arm and had her head buried in his side. And the thought occurred to Lucien—

If I am killed, the throne will go to Viceroy Lamont, by Royal decree.

Sterling will murder them all…

The strong men attached two of the chains to heavy iron rings set into the walls of the arena. The men backed away slowly and left the arena floor. If the dragon's strength was spent, those men did not believe it.

Raynard, his second-in-command, and Lord Sterling back away as well. The people who remained cheered for Lucien. Most of the seats, especially those nearest the dragon, were empty.

Lucien took a deep breath and gripped the sword with both hands. He reconciled himself to his impending death and stepped forward. The dragon looked down at his single attacker. It strained again at the chains and whipped its head about. Two heavy rivets that held the muzzle over its jaws shot into the air. And then, a third. And a fourth. The dragon wrenched his head back and forth at a dizzying speed.

The heavy leather muzzle ripped apart and fell to the arena floor. The dragon raised its head to the sky and opened its jaws wide.

One tiny blast of flame, and the dragon's fire was no more.

It tried to roar but produced only pitiful sounds of defeat.

Some members of the crowd laughed out loud. Some even made sounds of pity.

This made Lucien furious. He cursed at the

dragon until the dragon looked down at him. The dragon opened its jaws again and made no sound at all. Lucien lunged with his sword. The dragon moved. Lucien fell forward and the blade sliced into the dragon's leg. The dragon screamed and fell forward. Lucien rolled away just in time. The dragon's head slammed into the ground as it gave its final cry. Lucien ran the sword through the dragon's neck.

There was no roar left in the crowd—only a smattering of applause. Raynard ran to Lucien and pulled him to his feet. Lucien looked up at the Royal platform. He saw Jaclyn, being comforted by her parents. She held her hands to her face as she cried. Lucien pushed away from his uncle and ran to her. Sterling swore and walked after Lucien. Before Lucien reached Jaclyn, she turned away and ran.

"I will come with you, my queen," Helena said.

"No! Stay here, I command you!" Jaclyn said.

Jaclyn ran behind the platform and grabbed the reins of the first horse she came to. She tried to mount it but her ceremonial gown was too heavy and cumbersome. She screamed and ripped the gown away. Clad only in her undergarments, Jaclyn threw herself onto the back of the horse and dug in her heels. She yanked on the horse's mane, sending them along the King's Road at full speed.

Lucien ran to Lord and Lady Lamont.

"Where is she?" he asked, breathlessly.

"We do not know—"

Sterling caught up with Lucien and grabbed his arm from behind. Lucien wrestled his arm away.

"Where is Jaclyn?" Lucien demanded.

Sterling glared at Lucien, and then he glared at the Lamonts.

Sterling reached and grabbed Helena by her arm.

"Perhaps your queen has never learned of the pain and suffering that dragons brought to these lands!" Sterling sneered. "Look around you! It seems that many in this village have forgotten the days of death and fire! Perhaps, the queen believes they should be allowed to breed, and begin their reign of terror all over again!"

Helena tried to get away from Sterling's grip, but he squeezed harder. Helena cried out in pain.

"I'll tell you who should be breeding," Sterling spat. "The King and Queen of this realm are responsible for the continuation of the Royal bloodline. And nothing is being done about it!"

Sterling threw Helena at Lucien. Lucien threw his arms out and caught her.

"You've spent years practicing to slay a dragon, Your Grace," Sterling said as he stared at Viceroy Lamont.

"Perhaps you need to practice producing an heir! Put a baby in the belly of the handmaid if that is the best you can do!"

Nicolas Lamont pushed his wife behind him. His lieutenant, Finn, put a hand on the hilt of his sword. Lamont shook his head at Finn and stepped forward.

"You have disrespected the Queen of the Realm, Lord Sterling. Your behavior is—"

Lamont stopped when the swords of Sterling, Raynard, and the First Knight swung in front of his neck.

Sterling cleared his throat.

"My behavior is....what?"

"Your behavior is quite clear," Viceroy Lamont said. He took a step backward.

"As is the knowledge of where the real power of the realm abides."

Sterling smiled. He leaned forward.

"A very astute observation, Viceroy Lamont. It is a very good thing that we have an understanding. Let us keep this between friends, shall we?"

TWENTY-FOUR

Boone lowered the spyglass. He breathed heavily. "Is that what I think it is?"

"It's a dragon, all right," Simon said. "What are they doing with it? That is the important question."

"Where did it come from?" Boone asked. "That is yet another question."

"It must have been hiding in the Southlands," Simon said. "Else it is likely that we would have crossed paths. If I was a real dragon that is where I would hide— far away from the King's Guard and his army."

"What do they mean to do?" Boone asked.

"They mean to slaughter it—in front of an arena full of people!"

"On the King's name day? But why?" Boone asked.

"This is Sterling's doing," Simon said. "I am certain of it. He means to stoke the fires of hatred. The poor beast will be made to suffer—because of me!"

"That is not necessarily true, Simon. Dragons were killing and laying waste to men long before you were born. The curse inflicted upon you is yours alone! You are not required to shoulder the weight of every dragon's evil deed."

"Perhaps that was all true—long ago," Simon said.
"But you have seen it yourself. They live and they die—
alone. They will never mate. The few that are left will be
the last. They have to hide to survive at all."
Simon pointed a talon.
"Look at that pathetic creature. I'll wager that he
has not eaten for days."
"Aye, that may be," Boone said. "But there is
nothing we can do about it. If there are five, or ten, or
twenty or more of them, we cannot save them—just as
we cannot save this one."
Simon said no more. He continued to stare up the
King's Road, and the spectacle of the dragon in chains
being driven forward at the point of a whip.

"We should go, Simon," Boone said. "There is
nothing we can—"
"Soon," Simon said. "Very soon, my friend."
Boone sighed and sat down with his back against
the wall.
"There is nothing we can do," he whispered to
himself.

The men and the dragon disappeared behind the
walls of the arena. The sounds of the crowd within the
arena rose. Boone stood and stepped next to Simon.
"I know this troubles you, my King. Why do you
torture yourself? Why don't we leave this place?"
Simon continued to stare at the arena walls though

he could see nothing. Boone stepped away and waited.

Movement on the King's Road caught Boone's attention. He raised the spyglass.

"Simon! Look!"

Simon climbed down from the wall.

"There! On the King's Road!" Boone said. "Riding away at full gallop—and…and clad only in her under—"

"That is Jaclyn."

"Now, do not allow your eyes to deceive you, Your Grace," Boone said. "It is most unlikely that the Queen is riding away from the arena in her undergarments—"

"I am not deceived," Simon said. "I would know her anywhere."

"Well, it is definitely time for us to go," Boone said.

"Yes, it is," Simon said.

"Climb on. I will take you to the cave, and then I am going to her."

"Going to her?" Boone said. "Have you lost your—?"

"Get on."

"Let us discuss this, Si—"

Simon glared at Boone. His eyes blazed with orange flame. He turned his head aside.

"NOW!" Simon barked. Flame shot from his mouth and struck the wall.

Boone climbed on.

Simon flew at such a speed that Boone could barely breathe. He held on so tightly his entire body became numb. Just when he reached the point he thought he would fall, Simon dove. He slowed and hovered over the ground. Boone slipped off. Without a word, Simon flapped his wings and shot into the sky. Boone fell from a distance of several feet, landing on his back. He groaned, rolled over, and climbed to his feet. He looked up and watched the dragon disappear into the clouds.

"Your mother, the sorceress, and now your brother's wife—the Queen. What a way you have with the ladies, my friend!" Boone said aloud. He stretched his arms and pushed a fist against the small of his back.

"We are going to die in such spectacular fashion!"

TWENTY-FIVE

Jaclyn buried her face in the horse's mane. Her eyes burned from the force of the wind — and her tears. She refused to allow the horse to slow down as they sped up the King's Road.

Jaclyn did not know where she was going, but she longed to be far away from Lucien and his evil, evil uncle —

And the dead dragon, who reminded her of the friend she had missed for five unbelievably long years.

The horse reared and whinnied. It came to an abrupt halt, forcing Jaclyn to throw her arms around the horse's neck.

Two large trees lay across the road — extending from one side of the forest to the other.

"This is my fault, I'm afraid."

Jaclyn jumped and shrieked when she heard the voice.

A long-forgotten, yet hauntingly familiar voice. The voice came from the forest.

"I wanted you to stop — but I did not want the

horse to rear and fall on you. That would be bad manners."

Jaclyn slid from the horse's back. She took one cautious step toward the trees. She leaned forward.

"It is YOU, is it not?"

"Your scaly old friend with the big teeth. Yes."

"And the…the wings?"

"Let me look…yes, I still have them," said the voice.

"Simon," Jaclyn whispered. "Are you going to come out where I can see you?"

"You should tie-off your horse. He will not like me."

Simon stepped onto the road.

"I have missed you," Jaclyn said.

"Aw, I wager that you say that to all the dragons."

Jaclyn giggled.

"And that is what I have missed most of all!"

Simon braced himself when he saw Jaclyn running at him. She threw her arms around him as best she could.

"Get away from her, foul creature!"

Nicolas Lamont and his lieutenant, Finn stood with bows taut—with arrows aimed at Simon's head.

"Father! No!" Jaclyn cried.

"Get away from it, Jaclyn," Lamont said. "Our arrows are aimed at the beast's eyes. At this distance, we cannot miss."

Jaclyn turned. She backed against the dragon's body and spread her arms to protect him.

"You will do no such thing!" she shouted. "I am the Queen! You will do as I say! Put down your bows!"

Finn kept his arrow aimed at the dragon's head as he shifted his weight between his feet. He was confused and conflicted, and looked toward Lamont for guidance.

"Jaclyn," Lamont said quietly. His bow remained steady. "I know what happened in the arena upset you, but—"

"He is my friend, Father!" Jaclyn cried. "My truest friend! If you want to kill him—you will have to kill me first!"

"Viceroy Lamont—I would die a thousand deaths before I harmed a hair on your daughter's head," the dragon said.

Finn's knees buckled, and he dropped his bow.

"Great Vehallion's ghost!" Nicolas Lamont whispered. He lowered his bow.

"You can speak!"

"Of course, he can speak, Father," Jaclyn said. "He was meant to be King! And he speaks the language of a King!"

"But you must understand, Jaclyn. It is cursed— and hunted by every swordsman in the realm—!"

"That does not make it right!" Jaclyn said. "Simon

bears no responsibility for the curse—as he bears no responsibility for those that rule in his stead! The Kingdom has fallen to the wicked—Lord Sterling may as well declare himself to be King and Queen!"

There was a rustling in the trees. Lamont caught Finn's eye and nodded toward where the sound had come. Finn drew his sword and circled around. He disappeared into the forest.

"You speak the truth, my daughter—and my Queen," Lamont said. "But the truth changes nothing. The Morgenwraithes have beaten the people down and destroyed any hope that the state of tyranny can be overthrown. This has gone on now for four generations, and it is Lord Sterling's every intention to keep it that way. Your husband is King in name only. He is but a boy! A frightened boy."

"And that boy now knows that a dragon will bleed—and die," Simon said. "While his subjects cheer and chant his name."

"If you make it a practice to attend these ceremonies, you will not be long for this world," Lamont said. "What is it you hope to achieve? Did you learn nothing the night that my men tried to kill you at Islemar? Do you plan more of your little midnight chats with the Queen—until you are caught and both of your heads end up displayed on the castle walls?"

"I have stayed away for five years, My Lord—"

"And you should stay away for five more!" Lamont snapped.

"I told you that Simon is my friend, Father,"
Jaclyn said. "Does that mean nothing to you?"

Lamont breathed heavily and his shoulders
slumped.

"I truly wish it could be that simple, my love. But I
am thinking only of your safety—and the safety of our
people. You may not yet realize it, but your status as
Queen is important to so many. Our family, the people of
Islemar—they all sleep well at night because you sit at
the right hand of the King.

"Jaclyn, if it was ever discovered...

"Do you have you any idea how difficult it was to
keep word from getting out that this....this....thing was
visiting our home—"

Jaclyn began to cry.

"He is not a Thing!" she croaked. "He is a boy
who had his birthright stolen from him! A boy who
would have put an end to the murderous and evil ways
of his ancestors!"

"And should you be caught with him," Lamont
said, "his family will take your head. And his. Soon after,
they will take mine, and your mother's. And our
homeland—our home, Jaclyn, will become just another
abomination."

More rustling came from the trees.

A young man, dressed in dark work clothes,
stumbled onto the road. Finn walked behind him,
holding a handful of the young man's hair. The point of

Finn's sword was at the man's back.

"Well, look what I have found, My Lord," Finn said. "The forest has eyes and ears."

Finn marched the young man closer to the dragon. The man tried to break free and run, but he found Nicolas Lamont's sword at his throat.

Lamont glared at the young man.

"Who is he?"

"A Royal stable boy, so he says," Finn said.

"How did he get here so quickly?"

"He is either about the King's business, or he has stolen a Royal horse," Finn said.

"I am going to lower my sword," Lamont said to the young man.

"Do not move. This has been a very, very bad day."

Lamont turned to Jaclyn.

"Do you recognize this man?"

"Yes," Jaclyn said.

"What do you know about him—other than he possesses knowledge of horses?"

Jaclyn stared at the ground.

Nicolas Lamont put his finger under his daughter's chin and lifted her head.

"This is most important, my Queen."

"He whispers to Lord Sterling," Jaclyn said.

"No!" the young man cried.

Lamont lifted his sword again.

"Lord Sterling asks after my sisters—and my cousins!"

"Liar!" Jaclyn screamed. "Sterling does not ask after girls! He takes them! And he does with them whatever he wishes!"

"Boy," Lamont said. "Do you know the penalty for lying to the Queen, and to a Kingdom's Viceroy?"

"I am not lying, My Lord! I will say nothing to anyone! Your secrets will go with me to my grave!"

"So, you admit that you followed the Queen on the order of Lord Sterling in order to report back to him?"

"Yes....well, no—I mean..."

"Turn aside, Jaclyn," Lamont said softly.

"What?" Jaclyn said. "No. What do you mean to—? I will not turn away and hide from the ugliness of this world. This is my Kingdom!"

"Please, Jaclyn," Lamont whispered.

"No, Father, I will—"

Everyone jumped when the dragon unfurled his wings. He carefully wrapped them around Jaclyn.

"No, Simon!" Jaclyn said weakly.

She stretched her arms around the dragon and laid her head against his belly.

"I swear on my blessed mother," the stable boy moaned. "I would never—!"

Those were the stable boy's last words. Nicolas Lamont shoved his knife blade into the young man's throat.

"Let us get him onto your horse," Lamont said to Finn. "Do away with the body where it will not be found. Return to Morgenwraithe. Tell Lady Lamont that I ordered you back to attend to her before we caught up with Jaclyn."

"What about his horse?" Finn asked.

"Untie it," Lamont said. "It will find its way home."

TWENTY-SIX

Finn disappeared down the King's Road.

Simon unfurled his wings. Jaclyn lowered her arms.

"Jaclyn," Lamont said. May I have a private word with your friend?"

Jaclyn nodded and stepped away.

Lamont took three steps toward the dragon. He looked up.

"Thank you," he said.

Simon nodded.

"I will not let her be hurt—in her body, her heart, or her mind."

"How did you form such a strong bond with my daughter? You could not have met with her more than a few times."

"Did you never ask her?" Simon asked.

Lamont turned and looked at Jaclyn. She had her back turned.

"She would not speak to me for quite some time," Lamont said. "So many times, I found her crying. I tried to comfort her, but she would only look at me and ask 'why?' 'Why did you kill my friend?' It broke my heart."

"What do you wish me to say?" Simon asked.

"You choose a difficult path," Lamont said. "If you care deeply for both the queen and the king."

"I only know of my brother as a baby," Simon said. "Thus far, his reign as king speaks for itself."

"He has had no chance to do anything other than obey Lord Sterling," Lamont said.

"It is my hope to one day—" Simon began.

"You hope to one day do what? To break this curse, somehow? Is this your plan?"

"Yes, it is, My Lord," Simon said. "Perhaps it seems hopeless to you and to everyone else—but it is all that I think about. What else do I have? Every long day and every endless night. Yes. It is my plan. And I will see it come to pass, or I will die in its pursuit."

Lamont nodded.

"I admire your dedication. And your will. But how would we be assured that your reign would be any different from what we have now? You are still a Morgenwraithe. The blood of ruthless tyrants runs in your veins."

"That is true, Viceroy. My first order of business would be to return to the surname that belonged to my family since the dawn of time."

Lamont narrowed his eyes.

"Sterling would kill you for even speaking such a thing."

Simon laughed.

"Sterling needs no more incentive to kill me!"

"Any man in the Realm would be put to death for even mentioning the former surname of the Morgenwraithes," Lamont said.

"You know the name, then?" Simon asked.

"Smyth," Lamont said.

"Very good," Simon said. "The name says so much about our past, does it not? Ten years of building weapons to outfit an army strong enough to overthrow a King's Guard, a King's Army, and turn away a weak group of allies. My family has a glorious heritage, don't you think?"

"Many in my family were slaughtered in those wars," Lamont said.

"And good people they were, I am most certain," Simon said. "You must see why breaking this curse is my obsession, Lord Lamont. I care nothing about tournaments and parades, robes and thrones. I care about the Kingdom being ravaged by wicked men while I hide from swords and arrows."

Lamont looked down at the ground.

"I cannot reconcile myself to hearing such noble words from the mouth of a beast. They say that you take human form for one day—at the full moon."

Simon said nothing.

Lamont stared up at him.

"I would very much like to look you in the eye when you are a man."

"My heart is the same regardless of the skin I

wear. And so is my mind."

"I believe that," Lamont said. He turned aside.

"I cannot help you. I would very much like to see the wretched curse broken, but there is much at stake. I have too much to risk."

"I understand, My Lord," Simon said.

"Thank you, again, Simon Morgen—Simon Smyth."

"I hid her eyes from pain, My Lord. Nothing more."

"No. You have given her the one thing that no one else can.

"Hope."

"We have to go, Jaclyn," Lamont said. "Others will be coming."

"When will I see you again, Simon?" Jaclyn asked.

Nicolas Lamont grabbed the reins of his and Jaclyn's horses. He waited to hear Simon's answer.

"Your father is right. I…I should not have come here today. It is too danger—"

Jaclyn threw her arms around the dragon.

"I will never know another day without danger. I do not need an answer. I will see you again."

"Yes, my Queen," Simon bowed.

Lamont and Jaclyn mounted their horses and galloped up the King's Road, back toward the village and the castle beyond.

Simon took to the sky in the opposite direction.

The woman craned her neck and watched Simon disappear over the forest.

"What an amazing day," Magdalena whispered to herself.

She walked several paces toward the village. She saw a horse from the King's stable grazing beside the road. She tied up its reins so that they could not become tangled in the branches.

And then she leaned over and placed her hands on the ground.

Lady Magdalena, in the body of a wolf, ran for home.

TWENTY-SEVEN

"Boy!" Sterling growled.

"Yes, My Lord," the servant boy bowed his head.

Sterling sat in the Council chamber of Morgenwraithe castle. He shifted uncomfortably in his chair. The chair was designated for the king during official assembly, but Sterling took great pleasure in making it his own. He dared anyone to object. Sterling had never dared to sit upon the actual throne, but many people noted the lustful look in his eye whenever he entered the throne room.

"Fetch the Captain of the Guard!" Sterling barked at the boy.

"Do not return without him—and no less than three flasks of good wine. And bring one more taster with you. Make haste!"

The boy scurried away.

Raynard walked into the Council room and fell into a chair. He winced and stood. He loosened his sword belt and let his sword clatter to the floor.

"You seem quite tired, my friend," Sterling smirked.

"Tired? After overseeing the transport of a stubborn, old dragon for twenty miles? I should think so."

Raynard snatched a flask of wine from the servant boy's hand.

Sterling leaped up and grabbed it from Raynard's hand.

"Do not allow fatigue to cloud good judgment, Captain. Boy! Taste the wine—both of you!"

The two servant boys poured small amounts of wine into cups. They sipped the wine.

"Empty them! Drink them down!" Sterling yelled. "Act as if you may actually become men one day!"

The boys emptied the cups and stood nervously as Sterling and Raynard observed them.

"Ah, it is a good day," Sterling said. "Everyone lives. Now, get out!"

The boys were happy to do so.

"So, the Boy-King is now a ferocious dragon-slayer!" Raynard said as he massaged his temples. "That was not exactly your intended outcome, was it?"

Sterling leaned forward.

"Of course, not, you fool! And keep your voice down!"

Raynard dismissed Sterling's concern with a wave of his hand.

"What or whom do you have to fear, Sterling?"

Sterling leaned back and took a drink.

"Two years. Two years until his seventeenth name

day, and the dissolution of my position as Regent. That is not my fear. That is my immediate concern."

Raynard picked up his sword from the floor. He pulled it from its scabbard and held it before him. He sighted its edge.

"If only there was a simple solution..." he said.

"Bah!" Sterling slapped the table. "He is the last of the bloodline. If he dies, the throne goes to Lamont. We certainly cannot allow that to happen."

"Would that be so bad?" Raynard asked. "With Lamont here at Morgenwraithe, we could take complete control of Islemar. We could demand even more tariffs from the merchant captains. We could double our take! What choice would they have?"

"Your thinking is small—and short-sighted," Sterling growled.

"You do not remain in power with mere riches. You must have the power to keep your riches, and that is done through the spread of fear. A rich man cannot protect his wealth from the poor masses by having more riches. He protects his wealth by controlling the King's Guard and army."

"We may have to use that army, if the rumors of malcontent in the Southlands continue to reach my ears," Raynard said. "We have sent nothing there from the ships for most of a year. I do not feel bound to honor our treaty with those heathens any more than you do, but I do fear an uprising. Perhaps if we demand ten percent

more from the merchants, we could appease the South—
"

"Are you really that stupid?" Sterling said.
"Lamont knows nothing about what we take from his
merchant ships. The captains hold their tongues because
I threaten to cut them out. Lamont is held in high
regard—perhaps the most respected man in the realm. If
he were King, I would be arrested and beheaded. And
you would be next.

"Lucien must live. For now."

"Lucien fears you," Raynard said. "So, in two
years, you are no longer Regent. Why does anything
change after that day?"

"Let me ask you, Captain of the Guard." Sterling
said.

"If two years from today, your seventeen-year-old
King tells you to plunge your sword into my heart, what
will you do?"

Raynard stared at Sterling.

Sterling slapped the table again.

"That—is precisely what will change two years
from now!"

"Then what is the solution?" Raynard asked.

Sterling stood and paced the floor.

"Yes, there have been reports of grumblings from
the south. But none of the spies I have sent there report
any talk of a revolt. And for the most part, the different
villages do not even trust each other. This is no

environment in which to organize an army! I have sent word to them that we have suffered losses from storms and such."

"They will only believe these stories for so long," Raynard said.

"You said it yourself—they are heathens," Sterling said. "What would they use to attack us? Their women and children—armed with sticks and rocks? They would not get past the first line at our border! I have stationed a line of archers there, and the passage is lined with snares. I lose no sleep over the Southlands or its people."

"But you lose sleep over the King's seventeenth name day," Raynard said.

"The solution to that would be simple indeed," Sterling said. "Except that the womb of the Queen remains empty."

"Why does that matter?" Raynard asked.
Sterling smiled. A wicked smile.
And Raynard understood what Sterling meant.
"If Lucien has an heir. A living heir…"

Sterling smiled.
"The Kingdom could have need of its Regent for seventeen more years."

TWENTY-EIGHT

Magdalena stopped when she neared her front door. She sniffed the air.

There was someone inside her home.

She transformed back into human form and pushed her door open. She stepped inside.

"Your Grace," she said. "What a pleasant surprise."

Lucien stood up from the chair. Magdalena looked around the room.

"Surely, you are not alone. You have never been alone in any room other than a privy in your entire life!"

"It is time for that to change," Lucien said.

"Ah, the ever-important fifteenth name day! How silly of me to forget. I am not so certain that Lord Sterling will be thrilled by this new development."

"Sterling need not know everything, My Lady. And he cannot be everywhere."

"But, unfortunately, his eyes and ears can be," Magdalena said.

"Does this include yours?"

"It does not."

"Where have you been?"

"That is none of your concern," Magdalena said.

"I am only the King. Please, tell me more about the things that are not my concern."

Magdalena stepped across the room. She filled a cup from a pitcher of water.

"Would you care for a drink, Your Grace?"

"No."

"You were present, my King, at my inquisition before the Royal Council. You must know the futility of threatening me."

"I have been told my entire life, that no magic can be used against the throne of Morgenwraithe," Lucien said. "Is this true?"

"It has been true since—"

Lucien gripped his heavy gloves in his right hand. He swung them hard against Magdalena's cheek.

She stared at the floor and watched her blood drip at her feet.

"Lord Sterling has taught you well—"

Lucien dropped the gloves and grabbed Magdalena by the throat.

"If your magic would work against me," Lucien said, "I dare say my sleeve would be on fire right now."

Lucien continued to squeeze until the color drained from Magdalena's face. Her eyelids fluttered. Lucien let go.

Magdalena fell against the wall, gasping for air. She coughed.

"What do you want from me?" she croaked.

"It is not a matter of what I want. It is what I demand!" Lucien said.

"An ally."

"Ally?" Magdalena laughed. "How could I be more of an ally than I have already been? I cursed your brother and made you King! At what time have I failed to be your—"

"Whoever said I wished to be King?" Lucien screamed. "The people do not love me. They do not respect me. They only fear me—because my uncle is the spawn of hell!

The room fell silent.

"Lucien," Magdalena said, "what do you want from me?"

Lucien blew out a breath.

"I will never be a warrior. I will never lead my armies into battle. And I most assuredly cannot fight on two fronts."

"I do not understand," Magdalena said.

Lucien looked away.

"The law respects the authority of the King's regent until the King's seventeenth name day. Two more long years I remain under Sterling's thumb."

"Why does this concern you?" Magdalena asked.

"Perhaps it is only a feeling," Lucien said. "But I can think of little else of late."

"What does the dragon have to do with—?"

"Is it true?" Lucien asked. "What you said before the Council? That there is no way to know what would become of the dragon should you be...should you...die?"

Magdalena glared at Lucien, and then she dropped her eyes.

"After your mother proposed her plan to avenge herself, I sought the help of an old and half-mad potion-master. Two days after I invoked the curse, the old man fell dead."

"You never thought to inquire about the possibility of the curse being broken?" Lucien snapped.

"I was halfway mad with rage myself at the time! I did not expect to live for long after what we had done."

"And yet, you have not only lived—but you are the only person in the realm that Sterling holds no power over!"

"Why do you concern yourself with your brother? With each passing year, he becomes less human, and more animal. Why do you not simply ignore him?"

"Do you think I am not aware of the peoples' whispers? Of how I am nothing more than Sterling's puppet? And that many people wonder if your curse cheated them out of their true King?"

"You heard the true thoughts of the people today—inside the arena," Magdalena said. "Few people have forgotten the days of terror—when dragons filled our skies. Their legend grows even more terrible in their absence! A young mother may have never seen a dragon in her lifetime, but when she hears the tales of a dragon stealing babies from their mother's arms, they carry that fear with them always. Tales of burned homes and destroyed crops become even more terrifying when told by the light of a fire.

"Your mother devised the near perfect curse, Lucien. Who might have guessed that she could become so intensely jealous of your father's love for your brother—?"

"Be silent!" Lucien screamed. "What makes you think I wish to hear your interpretation of our past?"

Magdalena bowed her head.

"Forgive me. I thought we were speaking in confidence."

Lucien stared out the window.

"I fear him."

"There is no shame in fearing such a deadly beast," Magdalena said.

"I am not afraid of death—even by talon or fire," Lucien said. "I fear Sterling because he has owned me since I was far too young to do anything about it. He has used his position as Regent to amass more power than I will ever have."

"Then what is there to fear from Simon?" Magdalena asked.

Lucien turned to look at her.

"I fear him because of his goodness. I fear him because...because whatever happened to strip the madness from our bloodline began with him."

Lucien turned away again.

"Simon was remarkable at an early age—but so was I. I was also a miserable child. I remember…hurting. My head always hurt. And my neck. But I was too young to tell anyone.

"I can remember as early as my third year— listening to the maids and servants as they whispered to one another. It never occurred to them I was listening and understanding their words. They spoke of Simon as though he was a god. Intelligent. Witty. Brilliant. Kind. Thoughtful. Delightful.

"They adored him. How could I ever convince myself that the people would not have loved him as their King?"

Lucien glared at Magdalena.

"But your splendid curse took care of that!"

"The curse gave you the throne."

"I did not want it!"

Magdalena clutched at her heart. The words sounded like they came from a frightened child.

Because they had.

"Nevertheless, my King," Magdalena whispered. "It is your fate, now. Perhaps Simon will accept his fate and stay far away from here. He can live to a ripe old—"

"He has to die," Lucien said.

"You said yourself—he is intelligent," Magdalena said. "He knows that—"

"He recently had his hand around your throat, if I

remember your words correctly," Lucien said. "He has a friend—an ally. One does not need an ally to hide in mountain caves."

"Perhaps he—"

"Your speculation means nothing! He shadows the Kingdom because he seeks to break the damned curse!"

Magdalena reached out. She touched Lucien's sleeve.

"You do not want the throne. What if…what if the curse was broken—?"

Lucien jerked his arm away.

"Are you mad? Your treachery cannot be undone, Witch! Even if the curse was broken and every citizen of the realm called for Simon to take the throne—where would that leave me? Sterling would cut me into pieces!"

Magdalena shook her head.

"Simon cannot have any realistic hope of taking the throne, Your Grace. It is impossible. The sensible thing for him to do is what I have said. To stay far away."

"He will not stay away," Lucien said. "And he will never give up. Never."

"How can you know such a thing?"

"Because I wouldn't."

TWENTY-NINE

Boone watched as Simon approached the small clearing near their cave. Boone ran to meet him.

"I thought you would be fast asleep," Simon said.

"Surely, you jest," Boone said. "What happened? Did you see the Queen?"

"The Queen—and her father," Simon said.

"Her fath—I swear that you have a death wish. Please, tell me you did not speak to them!"

"Well, her father and another soldier under his command held arrows pointed at my eyes, so I felt it the appropriate thing to do."

"Is this story true?" Boone asked.

"Partially. The 'arrows at the eyes' part is most definitely true."

"If I know you at all, that is the only reason you did not land here with the Queen on your back," Boone said.

"The Queen did save my life today. It would only be fair of me to return the favor."

"I was not aware that the Queen was in need of saving. Have they drastically limited her number of servants? Is the cushion on her throne too hard to bear?"

Simon snorted.

"Jaclyn is not like that, Boone. She is good-hearted and noble—much like her father. Lady Jaclyn never wanted to be Queen."

Boone bit his lip.

"What have you kept hidden from me, Simon? I have kept no secrets from you. Until tonight, I thought you kept no secrets from me.

"I thought—I thought we were friends."

"We are friends," Simon said.

"Then why did you never tell me about—?"

"Because I was ashamed!" Simon growled. Smoke rolled from his jaws. He blinked—several times.

"I met her at her family home, on the night of her brother's wedding. I could say our meeting was by chance, but that would be a lie. I saw her—and I could not turn my eyes away. Though I knew that she was to wed my brother, I was…."

"Helpless."

"I am sorry that you felt you could not share this with me," Boone said.

"I went back, the next night," Simon said. "But she was not there. I scolded myself for my stupidity—but the next night I flew there again. And she was waiting for me. But after only minutes, Jaclyn's father and his men stormed into the room. They almost….they almost killed me."

"So, your heart got the best of your head," Boone

said. "That certainly was not the first time that this has happened, Your Grace. You were a young boy with perfectly normal—"

"Don't you see, Boone? I put Jaclyn in danger—not merely that night—but every night since. What if word had reached Sterling that I was making social calls to the Viceroy's home? And the home of the future Queen? How could I ever explain being so foolish while still being determined to obtain the throne?"

Boone said nothing.

"Sometime I believe I can feel it, Boone," Simon said. "The blood. The very blood that bears the madness of generations of Morgenwraithes—coursing through my veins! Simon Smyth! The dragon who wants to be King! The dragon that is in love with—!"

Simon stopped talking. His jaw hung open.

Boone leaned back against a tree. He puffed out his cheeks and blew out a long breath.

"You…love her, Simon?"

Simon did not look at Boone.

"I was thirteen years old, as was she. The night I first saw her, she was so lovely it tore at my heart to stay away. And now—her beauty knows no limits, Boone. And she has the heart of an angel. But I remain trapped inside of this curse. And the Lady Jaclyn Lamont has become my Queen, and my brother's wife."

Simon stretched his wings and then stretched his neck.

"I have been hungry enough to eat an entire horse.

I am able to kill a man and swallow him in two bites. Yet, my feelings for one girl leave me as helpless as a field mouse."

"You could have told me all of this before, you know," Boone said.

Simon laughed.

"Perhaps so. It does feel better to have bared my soul."

"Maybe you have failed to realize that I am a bit of a romantic, myself," Boone said.

"And what evidence might have ever given me that idea?" Simon asked.

"Ha, ha! Evidence, you say? I'll tell you this, Your Grace. Should you ever show up with the Queen on your back, you had better have her lovely handmaid with you, as well!"

"I wouldn't have it otherwise," Simon said. What was her name a—?"

"Helena," Boone said.

"You had that name on the end of your tongue, didn't you?"

"You bet I did!"

"Yet another chapter in our tale, my friend," Simon said.

"When you recount the day to the minstrels, you might leave out the part about eating the horse."

"A bit too much, you think?" Simon asked.

"Might be a bit much for the squeamish. Nothing spoils a good romantic tale like people vomiting on each other."

"I'll have to take your word on that," Simon said. "I have not been to a party since I was six."

"That reminds me," Boone said. "I got you something—for your name day."

"It is not my name day."

"Well, then, for your brother's name day," Boone said. "I ran into a herd of wild boar. They seemed interested in having me for dinner. I barely escaped up a tree in time, but I did manage to sink my knife into one of them. That doesn't exactly amount to a feast for a big fellow like you, but..."

Simon laughed.

"Thank you, Boone. The boar will be plenty. I plan to rise early and search out a hunting party to scavenge from."

"I'm beginning to wonder if you do that more for amusement than to get something to eat," Boone said.

Simon launched into the air before sunrise. He did not have to fly far before he heard the sound of trumpets. That is always a good sign, he thought to himself.

Trumpets at dawn usually accompanied a large hunting party. A large hunting party meant that an advance team of scouts had located the very best prey.

Simon circled the area and took cover in the forest. As always, he looked for the dogs.

There were a dozen of them that morning—more

dogs than he had ever seen used on a hunt.

I wonder what grand prize may lie in store this exceptional morning, Simon thought.

The dogs were loosed. Simon waited for the hunters to follow them. He took to the skies and circled ahead of the dogs. He flew low over the edge of the forest until he spotted the object of the hunt.

Four head of bison.

Simon could not help himself. He salivated. A flood of memories from his youth ran filled his mind. The magnificent feasts—the reasons for which he never knew or cared about. Heaping platters of his favorite foods, the greatest of which now stood huddled together beneath him. Bison.

The largest of the animals was easily over a thousand pounds.

But there was something wrong. The bison were not moving. At all.

Surely, they hear the dogs.

Simon flew closer—close enough to see that the bison were tied together and staked to a tree.

Fifteen archers stepped out, arrows pulled tautly and aimed at that morning's real prey—

Simon Smyth Morgenwraithe

The dragon.

Fifteen arrows flew as Simon reversed direction. The arrows caromed off of his scales. One of them struck a wing tip and passed straight through.

Behind those fifteen archers stepped fifteen more.

Simon banked and turned toward his nearest line of escape—a narrow passage between two stands of trees. If he could just make it through, he could separate himself from the archers enough to elevate without exposing his neck and belly.

Thirty archers? Simon thought. In designed formation—as if they were at war...

Simon tried to stop, but he had no chance.

Just as he was on the verge of escape, he saw what awaited him between the trees.

A snare.

THIRTY

The snare tore loose from the trees from the dragon's weight and the speed of his flight. It pulled against Simon's body and rolled him into a ball. He blew a blast of fire but the flame had nowhere to go but into his own vulnerable belly.

Simon looked down at the rope snare. It was unscathed.

Bewitched. I should have known.

Simon hit the ground. His momentum caused him to roll. The ropes gripped him tighter and tighter as he slowed to a stop. He lay on his side, staring into the forest. Two bluebirds hopped among the branches and stared at him.

How will it happen? Simon thought. Will my life leave me as I stare at these birds? Or will my killers look into my eyes while their swords and arrows drain the tainted blood from my body?

"You are not nearly as frightening, balled up on the ground."

It was a pleasant voice—a young male voice that

bore the dialect of the wealthy and powerful. It was not a familiar voice. It did not sound like the voice of one who was accustomed to slaughter—especially after initiating a discussion.

"It would be difficult to appear frightening while completely at the mercy of one's enemy," Simon said.

"He speaks, and he possesses above average intelligence," the voice said. "I can now confirm all rumors to be true."

"It seems that the day may be counted a success—for one of us," Simon said.

"Go back!" the voice said. "Go back and join the others!"

"But, my K—"

"Did I not speak clearly?" the voice asked. "Do you wish to wake in the morning with your head attached to your shoulders?"

Simon heard the scurrying of feet.

Simon struggled to breathe. A pair of boots appeared in front of his eyes. Someone knelt in front of him.

"It has been a long, long time, Brother."

"Lucien?"

"To tell you the truth, I thought you would be smarter than to continue raiding hunting parties," Lucien said. "Is it simple arrogance?"

"No," Simon said.

"Then why do you continue to do it? Why put

yourself in such a dangerous position—in reach of
arrows that might strike you down at any time? Is there
some special thrill that comes from stealing a man's kill
that I am not aware of? You have every means available
to fill your belly at will. Speed, agility, talons, fire—why
tempt fate as you do?"

"I only live if others die," Simon said.

Simon breathed out. A tiny flame burst from one
nostril. Lucien jumped back.

"I am being foolish," Lucien said. "Your jaws are
bound tight, but it seems that you still present a danger."

"Is that what you believe, Lucien?" Simon said.
"Do you believe that I would starve myself to avoid
killing—and yet still be willing to harm my...my baby
brother?"

"I am truly sorry, your Grace," came another voice
behind them. "I...I could not stop him. The Captain of
the Guard approaches."

Lucien looked at Simon. Simon saw the King
swallow hard—his eyes clouded in confusion.

Lucien stood.

"I want it brought to the castle," Lucien said. "Put
it on the cart. I want it unharmed."

"Yes, your Grace. He is bound tightly now,
but...what if the dragon is able to...to make fire?"

"The sorceress constructed the snare, Sire," Lucien
said. "But I would recommend that you avoid the beast's
head."

"Yes, your Grace."

The King's men brought on a large cart and a lift with which to lift the snared dragon.

They have prepared this—for how long? Simon thought.

He swore at himself under his breath for his naive stupidity—and his brash disregard for the King's planning and tenacity. He used words that were only a distant memory—words he had heard his father and uncle use on occasion. This only made him feel worse.

Simon only caught the occasional glance of a leg or foot while he lay motionless curled into a fetal position. He watched the legs of men skirting around to avoid his mouth as they tied him up with heavy ropes.

Soon, Simon lay in that same position of the bed of the cart. With a lurch, the cart began its bumpy journey.

Why did he not just kill me and get it over with? Simon thought. But he knew the answer.

His death would be a ceremony. He would become the next "spectacle"—in the same way as the last dragon.

In the arena—and in front of the entire Kingdom.

A spectacle of might, and cruelty. Dominance and power. Orchestrated and ruled over by Lord Sterling.

Cheered on by a people ruled by fear and intimidation. A people without hope.

The people's last hope rolled onto the King's Road atop a battered wagon. The boy dragon, who would be

King, felt his own hope fade away as a single giant tear splashed against the wooden deck.

THIRTY-ONE

Drip. Drip. Drip.

Simon opened one eye. He ached all over. Water dripped in front of him in three different streams.

The snare was gone. He was now chained against a wall. He had only vague and distant memories of the dungeon beneath Morgenwraithe castle. Simon assumed, correctly, that that was where he was. He worked his jaw open and closed several times. He was surprised that his jaws were not clamped shut. He was glad of it, but did not for a moment believe it was a good thing.

The explanation for the lack of head restraint stood before him — in the form of a ten-foot-tall shield made of thick steel.

As he looked over the chains and shackles, someone stepped from behind the shield.

"You're awake. Good," the sorceress Magdalena said.

"I did not rest well, if that is your next question," Simon said. "I am bound securely — in the dungeon of my family home. Why am I not muzzled?"

Magdalena pointed at the curved steel wall.
"Because of this."
"I do not remember that. What is it?"

"It was found in the castle of a rival Kingdom,"
Magdalena said.
"Of course, Sterling sees everyone as rivals. No
one knew what the thing was until some of the family
members were interrogated. It is a Dragon Shield."
"Dragon shields are nothing new," Simon said.
"In that particular village, dragons were captured
and chained to the dungeon wall—in the same manner as
you are. They were teased, prodded, and tortured until
their anger and frustration overcame their ability to
reason. When they loosed their fire in front of this shield,
it came right back upon them. A demented form of sport
if you ask me—but highly effective."
"You feel no need to hide behind its protection, I
see."
Magdalena held her arms out to her side.
"As you once said to me, our lives are intertwined.
You don't like it, but you do not really wish to see me
dead."
She lowered her voice.
"Just as I do not wish for you to die."

"Why are you here?" Simon asked.
"I was charged with making sure you remained
unconscious while they moved you from the wagon to
this place. You made quite the impression on the men of
the King's Army. You threatened to wake up twice, and I

watched several grown men soil themselves. You should be proud."

"I should be proud? You created a dragon, and the Kingdom depends on you to assure that I can harm no one."

"I had no guarantee of success," Magdalena said. "I have never sedated anything larger than a man. I could just as easily have killed you—or left you a helpless cripple."

"Forgive me if I cannot applaud your efforts. I am unable to bring my hands together," Simon said. "I am also currently fixated on the fact that I shall soon die, horribly."

"You will die, because you have been a fool!" Magdalena spat.

"Foolish and arrogant! Invading my home with your demands! Mocking parties of trained and experienced hunters! When you die, the fault will be your own."

The dragon sighed.

"My Lady," said a voice beyond the corridor. Magdalena looked over her shoulder.

"He is alive. And awake. There appears to be no physical damage."

Magdalena looked at Simon and glared.

"And his mind is still quite sharp."

Magdalena left the dungeon. Lucien stepped in, warily. He stood beside the protective shield.

"So, it is over, at last," Simon said.

"Yes, it is," Lucien said. "Our dear Uncle Sterling lives and breathes—"

"And drinks, and rapes and—"

"I am not under burden to defend him, Brother-Dragon!" Lucien spat. "I am certain you think of nothing but your own innocence at six years of age. How much responsibility should I have borne at the age of three?"

Simon slowly turned his face away from Lucien.

"He is only a man. You will not remain a boy forever, Lucien. You must prepare—"

"Hold your tongue!" Lucien cried. "Do you really have no idea what the throne has been reduced to?"

"I know Sterling has abused his position as Regent to—"

Lucien laughed.

"Abused? Abused his position? No man in the realm has been more feared since the days that our ancestors first breached these walls! He rules the King's Guard with an iron fist—and the army commanders, as well. He has built a powerful circle of allies, which he rewards handsomely from the Kingdom coffers. And worse yet, he is regularly convinced that all neighboring Kingdoms have become threats to the realm."

Lucien paused. He looked down and continued softly.

"We have slaughtered entire villages—in my name. Decrees of war bearing my seal have brought about the death of thousands. I may as well have committed each murder with my own hands."

"You need help, Lucien. Allies. This situation does

not have to—"

Lucien clamped his hands to his ears.

"Shut your mouth! Shut it, I say!" Lucien screamed. "You do not know, Dragon! You have no idea of the evil that man possesses! I was ten, Simon! A mere boy of ten on the day he knelt before me with his stinking breath in my face and his hand around my neck. I had embarrassed him! I had shamed him! I have feared the man every day of my life, but on that day I learned the unabashed truth.

"I am one blade—one arrow—one vial of poison away from death—at the hand of my own uncle."

"Islemar will be next," Simon said.

Lucien's head snapped up.

"What? What did you say?"

"Islemar will be the next village that Sterling seeks to destroy," Simon said.

Lucien stepped closer.

"How can you know—where did you hear this? Did the sorceress tell you this?"

Simon's belly growled. It growled again in quick succession.

"Tell me! Where did you hear—?"

"Lucien—"

"I demand that you answer me! Where did you hear—?"

"LUCIEN!" the dragon roared.

Lucien froze. His eyes bulged. He almost fell as he retreated to the edge of the shield.

"Lucien," Simon said calmly. "I have not burned

off the flames for some time now. When this happens, the source of the fire builds pressure in my belly. I must release it, or it will happen without any involvement of my will. I am going to turn aside now."

Lucien's jaw worked without a sound.

"You...you could have burned me alive, just now."

Lucien looked at the spot on the floor where he has stood just moments before.

"It would have happened instantly—it would have all been over."

Simon turned his head and blew fire across the empty air of the dungeon and into the far wall.

"There," he said. He turned his head.

"I do not want to kill you, Lucien. But, I must tell you. If it would save the realm from the future that lies before it now, I would."

"I know," Lucien said. "We could spend more time talking about what might have been. But Sterling will not let me out of his sight for much longer, so I will tell you what is going to happen tomorrow. Tomorrow is the full moon. We all know what that means. Before sunset, we shall assemble here. The Royal Counsel, The King's Guard, the first officers of the army, and the Royal scribes. After you transform into your man-self, you will be asked to officially deny all rights and claims to the throne of Morgenwraithe. At this point, regardless of your reply, you will be tried for High Treason. You will be judged, sentenced to death, and your head will be taken. We both know what Sterling will do with it after that."

Lucien walked away.

THIRTY-TWO

Lucien walked into the parlor. He found Jaclyn sitting in a chair, staring out the window. She turned when the door opened.

Her eyes were wet.

"Do you weep for the great fire-breathing beast?" Lucien asked.

He took off his cloak and threw it on the bed.

"Perhaps you listen to the peasants when they whisper that the Realm has been cheated of its rightful King."

"Lucien, I have never said—"

"You might be better served to listen to the rumors that a certain village has gathered the undesirable attention of the King's Regent!"

Jaclyn held her breath. She stood and walked close to Lucien.

"What are you saying, Lucien?"

Lucien grabbed her arms and pushed her away.

"I have had quite enough of your disrespect. You will no longer use my given name, as though we were two children frolicking in the fields. I am 'My King' or 'your Grace'. "

"What village do you speak of, your Grace?" Jaclyn wrung her hands.

Lucien stepped to another chair and fell into it. He stared out the window.

"Yours, of course."

"No!" Jaclyn cried.

She ran in front of Lucien and fell to her knees at his feet.

"Please, Lu—My King! You must speak to Lord Sterling! He mustn't—!"

Lucien pushed Jaclyn away again as he jumped to his feet. He faced away from her.

"Do not dare to tell me what I must do! I advise you to speak to your father. Perhaps he will be able to humble himself before Sterling in a sufficient manner— before it is too late."

"What is to become of…the dragon?" Jaclyn asked.

"Tomorrow's moon will be full," Lucien said. "When it becomes a man—"

Jaclyn put a hand to her mouth and shrieked. Lucien scowled.

"When it becomes a man, he will be asked before a tribunal to renounce his claim to the throne. And then, he will be tried for treason."

"And he has been judged guilty already!" Jaclyn cried.

Lucien turned and slapped Jaclyn to the floor.

"Of course, he is guilty!" Lucien screamed.

"Would you have it another way?"

Lucien grabbed Jaclyn's arm and jerked her to her feet.

"Come!" Lucien screamed. "Let us go down to the dungeon and declare the dragon to be king! Do you know what happens next, My Queen? I am tried for treason and executed! Every member of your family is executed while you watch! And then you are tried and executed!

"Oh, won't it be grand?"

Tears ran down Jaclyn's face. She pulled at Lucien's hand.

"You're hurting me, your Grace," she whispered.

Lucien threw her to the floor.

"To hell with you."

He stormed out of the room.

Jaclyn had never known such misery. She drifted in and out of sleep, sitting in her chair.

She woke to a touch on her arm.

"Is there anything I can do for you, my Queen?" Helena asked. "Can I get you something?"

Jaclyn wiped her eyes.

"No. Thank you."

"I will turn down your bed," Helena said. "You must be very tired."

Jaclyn nodded.

Helena took a step. Jaclyn grabbed her hand. She sniffed and looked Helena in the eye.

"I have but two friends in the entire world."

Helena took Jaclyn's hand in both of her own.
"You are adored by everyone, My Queen. My
mother and father say that—"
"I have but two, true friends, in the entire world,
Helena. You are one—
"The other will die tomorrow."

Helena gasped.
"What are you saying, My Que—?"
"My name is Jaclyn. Please, call me Jac—"
"No! I cannot. Lord Sterling would cut out my
tongue, My Queen! Are you saying that you…you
know…the dragon?"
"Yes."
Helena's head fell into her hands. She wept
bitterly. Jaclyn put a hand on her shoulder. Helena
jumped.
"I am so sorry, My Queen. My heart breaks for
you."
Jaclyn wrapped her arms around Helena, and they
wept together.
"My heart has broken for you as well," Jaclyn said.
"These foul, evil men have taken everything from you—
for no other reason than their own selfish fears."

"I must go now, my Queen. I am expected in the
kitchen," Helena said.
Jaclyn wiped her eyes and nodded.

Jaclyn climbed into bed. She slept fitfully and
woke in the middle of the night. Lucien had not returned

to their bed. Jaclyn was not surprised. She sat up and stared into the darkness. She slipped out of the bed and lit a lamp. Jaclyn took her jewelry box from the dresser. She dumped the contents onto the bed and then pried out the false bottom. Inside, was the gift her father had given her on his first visit to the castle after the Royal wedding. The gift was given in secret and without words.

A slender, razor-sharp dagger.

She considered leaving the room. But she would have to carry a lamp, and there were so many guards it would be impossible to go unnoticed. She placed the dagger into a drawer of her wardrobe. She sat on the bed and put the jewelry back into the box.

Jaclyn jumped when she heard the door open. The jewelry spilled onto the floor.

"I startled you. I am sorry," Lucien said. He rushed to Jaclyn's side and took the jewelry box from her hands.

"I'll pick these up. It was my fault."

"It is not a problem, your—"

"I am sorry for the things I said," Lucien said. "And for...hurting you."

Lucien held up a locket.

"I will buy you more of these. A Queen should have enough precious things to cover herself, head-to-toe! We will go to the finest shops after—we shall go, very soon."

Lucien put the jewelry into the box and closed it.

"There. Come, it is time for bed. It has been an exhausting day."

Jaclyn lay on her side. Lucien put his arm over her and was snoring within moments. Jaclyn shuddered and told herself not to cry.

And she slept.

THIRTY-THREE

When Jaclyn woke up, Lucien was gone. She had slept past midday. She was disgusted with herself.

When Helena heard Jaclyn moving about she stepped into the room.

"Would you like me to draw your bath, My Queen?"

Jaclyn struggled to pull a hairbrush through her tangled hair. Helena took the brush and brushed Jaclyn's hair.

"No," Jaclyn said. "This is nothing clean about this day. Taking a bath would seem like an insensitive slap in the face."

"Yes, My Queen. You must be hungry. What would you like me to send word to the kitchen—?"

"No," Jaclyn said. "I am not hungry. Thank you. You may go, Helena."

Helena stood.

"I could stay—if it would help you to feel better."

Jaclyn smiled weakly.

"Thank you."

She stood.

"But today, you should stay as far away from me as you possibly can."

Helena's eyes grew wide.

"What does that mean?"

"If I live to see tomorrow, we shall discuss it then. Go, now. Say nothing."

Helena shook her head furiously. She left the room in a hurry.

Jaclyn dressed and stepped out onto the balcony. She looked up to find the sun, but it was hidden in clouds. She did not know what time of day it was, and she did not mean to ask. She could not believe that soon, Simon Morgenwraithe, the rightful king and her friend, would be sentenced to die.

Jaclyn tried to appear as if everything was normal as she made a circuitous route to the dungeon. Her breath ratcheted from her when she reached the final corridor. She knew there was at least one guard between her and the dungeon door. She prayed that it was only one.

Jaclyn crept along the wall, changing sides to stay as far away as she could from the torches that lined the corridor. She reached the dungeon guard doorway and stopped. She took a deep breath and peeked around the door.

One guard. Asleep. His head back behind him.

Jaclyn slipped inside and drew the dagger. With a trembling hand she lifted the dagger to the guard's ear. She raised her other hand behind his head.

My life is now over. There is no turning back.

Jaclyn grabbed the man's hair at the same time she plunged the blade through his ear. It was over in an instant.

The guard fell to the floor. Jaclyn heard the ring of keys strike the floor. She grabbed them up and ran for the door. Several attempts later, her shaking fingers found the key that let her inside the dungeon.

The body of the dragon hung limply from the chains.

"No!" Jaclyn whispered a scream.

"Simon! Wake up! You cannot be dead! I will not allow it!"

"Jaclyn?" Simon raised his head. "What are you doing here?"

"Oh, thank the gods!" Jaclyn threw her arms around Simon. The keys clattered to the floor. Jaclyn grabbed them. She tried keys at the shackle around the dragon's neck.

"Jaclyn! What are you doing? Where is the guard?" Simon asked.

"I'm getting you out of here!" Jaclyn said.

"But…no, Jaclyn! It is not possible!"

Jaclyn fumbled the keys, and they fell to the floor again.

"I no longer care what is possible and what is not!" Jaclyn cried. She picked up the keys and returned to the shackle.

"Go back, My Queen," Simon pleaded. "Before it

is too la—!"

Jaclyn stopped only for a brief moment. She glared at Simon.

"It is already too late! They are coming! Before sunset! They are going to kill you!"

"I know all about it, Jaclyn," Simon said. "I have made peace with it, and you must as well. You must go now. They will not just kill you, Jaclyn—they will make you suffer. Sterling will make an example of you to the entire Realm! Your family—they will—!"

They both jumped when Helena burst through the door.

"What are you do—? I thought I would find you here!" Helena said breathlessly.

"My Queen," Helena pointed toward the corridor. "The guard—the guard is dead! Did...did you...?"

"Jaclyn, what have you done—?" Simon asked.

"It is true!" Helena whispered.

"He can speak!"

"You have to go, Helena!" Jaclyn pushed her away. "I command you to go n—!"

"The King is looking for you—I told him I had seen you walking in the garden," Helena said. "I do not think he believed me—please, my queen, you must come away now!"

Jaclyn continued to attempt to unlock the shackle at Simon's neck.

"No! I will not allow this to happen while I stand by and do nothing!"

Helena wrestled the keys away from Jaclyn. She threw them across the dungeon floor.

"I will not stand here and watch you slaughtered for nothing, My Queen. The King's men will be here any moment. It is over!"

Helena pulled Jaclyn from the room. Jaclyn drug her feet, but she was too despondent—and far too weak to struggle any longer. Their footsteps faded away up the length of the corridor.

THIRTY-FOUR

Simon closed his eyes. His head hung down. This hurt his neck a great deal—but he had no choice. All of his choices were a thing of the past.

Time had lost all meaning. He was still alive, but the inevitability of his death turned time into yet another enemy. That was the only thing he would see now until the moment of his death—

Enemies.

Simon heard footfalls in the corridor—coming nearer. Someone flashed into view and ran across the floor.

It was Helena.

She snatched up the keys from where she had thrown them and immediately went to work on the shackles.

"No, Helena…" Simon whispered.

Helena paid Simon no mind.

"Hold your tongue. You will need your strength."

"It is over," Simon said. "Leave—"

The first shackle fell open.

"I will tell you what is over, Dragon Prince. My future inside of this castle — that is what is over! These people murdered my family and left me a servant. To serve the Queen of the Realm is my only mission and purpose, and that is why I am here! Because the Queen only desires one thing."

Helena stopped momentarily and looked Simon in the eye.

"She wants you!"

Another shackle fell open. And then, another.

"I will stay here," Helena said. "When the King's men come, I will send them in the wrong direction."

One of Simon's wings and one of his legs were free.

"You will come with me," Simon said.

Helena swore at the last shackle. The key broke off inside the lock. The end of Simon's wing remained tethered to the wall.

Simon roared and jerked against the shackle. His other wing tore free.

"It will mend," Simon said.

There was shouting in the corridor. The door burst open.

"Get behind the shield!" Simon shouted.

Helena was confused. Simon pushed her with his wing. She tripped and fell. Simon stepped in front of her as twenty soldiers ran into the room.

The soldiers raised bows and swords. Simon knew

the time for thinking was over.

It was time — for war.

Simon opened his jaws and set fire to ten soldiers. He turned to the doorway and burned alive another wave of twenty.

Simon ran to the double doors. If he was to escape, it would be through these. The corridor of the main entrance was too narrow.

He ripped down the chains that held the doors closed. He threw his weight against them. The doors were secured on the outer side and did not budge.

Another wave of soldiers screamed down the main corridor. Simon moved behind the curved-steel shield. He put his shoulder against it and pushed. It barely moved.

Arrows flew through the open door.

Simon roared and charged at the shield. It fell over, blocking the main entrance.

"There is no way out for us, now!" Helena screamed.

"We will have to escape through the double doors," Simon said.

"But they are locked from the outside. You cannot open them!"

"I will not have to," Simon said.

They heard voices on the other side of the double doors. Something powerful and heavy hit the doors. Loud echoes filled the dungeon air.

"I have never been so frightened," Helena said.

"Neither have I," Simon said.

The soldiers on the floor of the dungeon were all
dead. Simon looked at each one. He found the smallest
one—who was also the least burned. Most of his face was
unmarked.

He was barely more than a boy.

Simon looked at Helena. He pointed a talon at her
neck.

"Your locket. Give it to me, please."

Helena put her hand around the locket.

"Why?" she whispered. "My mother gave it to me.
It is…all I have left to remember…"

"I'm sorry," Simon said.

Helena handed the locket to Simon. Simon placed
it near the dead boy's neck.

"Please, look away," Simon said.

Helena turned.

Simon opened his jaws and bathed the boy in
flames.

The body was unrecognizable. The locket lying
near its neck was charred, yet intact.

The sounds of rattling chains came from behind
the set of double doors.

"Hide behind the shield," Simon said. "Do not
move."

Both doors burst open and a wave of soldiers
pushed through them. Simon blasted the doorway with
fire. The screams made an awful chorus. The first wave

of men fell dead to the floor. The war cries of the next
wave grew louder as soldiers entered the wide corridor.

Simon stepped into the doorway and a wall of
flamed brought about more screams.

Simon's fire faded and then died altogether.

More men were coming. Their sound was distant.
Simon backed onto the dungeon floor.

"Close your eyes!" he screamed at Helena.

Dozens of charred, dead bodies lied at Simon's
feet. Without fuel, his fire died. And the war was lost.

He picked up a soldier in his jaws. He bit down
and severed the body in half. In two gulps, half of a man
disappeared. Two more bites and he felt the familiar
pressure building again within him as his belly swelled.

Another wave of men cleared the corridor — and
went to a fiery grave.

The last young man in the wave threw down his
sword. He turned to run. Simon chased him down and
caught him within five paces. Simon knocked the young
man into the wall.

"Please, no!" the man cried. "I am on your side,
King Simon!"

Simon raised his talon high — and left it there.

He lowered it.

"Go. Get out."

The man scrambled to his feet and ran.

Simon walked back into the dungeon. He walked
up to a dead soldier and kicked the helmet from his head.
He picked up a shield and the helmet and carried them to

Helena.

"Put this helmet on," Simon said. "And grab hold of this shield. If we are fortunate, they will have one more wave of foot soldiers to send before the King's Guard comes. We do not want to face them. After the next wave, we make our move. We escape—or we die."

Helena nodded. The helmet flopped loosely on her head.

The shouts of the next wave filled the corridor.

"I will clear the corridor," Simon said. "When I return, climb onto my back. Cover yourself with the shield the best you can. Hold tightly onto my neck."

The next wave was the last of the foot soldiers. It was a larger group, but they were paralyzed by fear. They turned and ran at the first sight of dragon fire.

Simon knelt down next to Helena. She climbed onto his back. Simon stepped into the corridor, lowered his head, and sprinted forward.

His memory of the area was distant. He was only allowed into the dungeon twice by the age of six— because in those days the dungeon was rarely empty.

Simon reached the end of the first leg of the corridor. He turned right and saw a light in the distance.

He heard shouting—the King's Guard was behind them. Flaming arrows flew past Simon on both sides.

"Hold on tight!" Simon yelled.

He stopped and spun around and filled the passageway behind them with fire. Helena lost her grip and fell to the floor. Simon leaned close to the floor, and

Helena climbed back onto his back.

"Please, hold on," Simon said. "The archers will be waiting for us outside. When we clear that door, I will take off and immediately bank to the north—to your right. You must hold on tightly, Helena!"

"I will," Helena said gruffly. She pulled the straps of the shield from her arm and let it fall to the floor.

"I cannot carry this…it is much too heavy."

Simon crept closer to the exit. He opened his mouth and filled the doorway with a quick blast of fire. He closed his mouth, saving his flame for their greatest challenge yet—the archers on the wall and in the north corner tower.

And then he ran.

The dragon and his rider exploded into the sunlight of late afternoon. The air filled with flying arrows and the screams of burning men.

Helena lowered her head and thought of nothing but holding on.

I have not come this far to die from hitting the ground, she thought.

Simon took flight and banked hard toward the north wall. The top of the wall was lined with archers. Simon angled toward them to shield Helena. He opened his jaws and forty men died instantly.

The last six men might have lived had they known the dragon's fire was almost spent. Instead, they threw themselves from the top of the wall.

Simon landed on top of the castle amid the litter of

smoldering bodies.

He glared at the watchtowers. They were all filled with archers. He dared not risk flying between any of the towers to escape. He had no time to replenish his fire. Already, more soldiers and King's Guard made their way to the top of the north wall.

"Helena," Simon said. "I need you to stay here. I must take out the threat in the north tower. I will be back for you."

Helena slid from Simon's back. She stepped onto a dead man's body. She screamed and jumped—and landed on the outstretched hand of another dead soldier.

Simon took to the air. He narrowed his eyes, staring at the largest window of the north tower. Archers crowded into that window and a flurry of arrows flew in Simon's direction. Without flame to spend. Simon flapped his wings as hard as he could. He lowered his head and flew at the window with all the speed he could obtain.

He collided with the stones on all sides, but his speed and his weight carried him through the window and inside the tower in a cloud of stone dust. Eight archers were killed instantly—crushed against the tower wall. Simon immediately spun in an offensive circle. Soldiers screamed and died in a fury of wings, talons and teeth. When only a few men remained alive, they chose the same fate as the men on the wall and jumped from the windows.

Simon returned to the wall. Helena climbed on

and they flew away, into the setting sun.

THIRTY-FIVE

The First Knight charged into the dungeon with his sword held high. He scanned the room and turned to leave. He ran past the door to the guard station and stopped. He looked inside and swore under his breath. And then he ran back up the corridor.

"The dungeon is clear," he said to those assembled there: Lucien, Sterling, Raynard, and several officers of the King's Guard.

"The guard was murdered—stabbed in the head."

Sterling screamed a string of obscenities and stormed toward the dungeon.

Raynard walked to the wall and stared at the empty shackles.

"These were unlocked with the key—save for one."

The men halted. Shouts came from the top of the corridor.

"Let go of me! I am your Queen! I will have your heads!"

Sterling looked at Lucien.

"Get her out of here!"

Lucien scowled and his hands became fists. He stomped up the corridor. Jaclyn had torn free from a member of the King's Guard, who was left holding the sleeve of her dress. Lucien stopped in front of her and held up his hands.

"You must remain here. There is nothing for a queen to see down—"

Jaclyn feinted to one side of the corridor and then ducked beneath Lucien's hands. She ran to the doorway of the dungeon with Lucien on her heels.

Jaclyn reached the doorway just as the First Knight bent over and lifted the locket off of the incinerated body.

"What have we here?" the Knight said to Sterling.

"No!" Jaclyn screamed.

Lucien grabbed her shoulder from behind.

"I told you to stay away—!"

"NO!" Jaclyn screamed again in anguish.

She jerked away from Lucien with all of her might. She freed one of her arms and threw her elbow backward. The blow struck Lucien's nose, breaking it, and sending blood into the air. Lucien fell to his knees.

Jaclyn ran to the body where the Knight found the locket. She fell to her knees in front of it.

"NO! Helena! NO!"

Raynard grabbed Jaclyn by the arm and jerked her to her feet.

Sterling stormed in front of her. It took every bit of his restraint not to strike her.

"Get her out of my sight!" He growled.

Raynard and another guard dragged Jaclyn from the dungeon, dragging her feet and screaming and sobbing.

"Wait!" Sterling said. "Keep her there!"

Sterling grabbed the locket from the First Knight's hand.

"Lucien!" Sterling yelled. He looked at the other soldiers.

"Where is he?"

A guard ran inside the dungeon.

"The king is in the corridor, my Lord. He is injured."

"Get him in here! Now!"

Two guards held Lucien at the elbows and helped him through the dungeon doorway. They walked past the guards and Jaclyn, who continued to sob.

Sterling held the locket in front of Lucien.

"Do you know this locket?" he asked.

Blood flowed from Lucien's nose. The skin around his eyes was turning black and swollen. He squinted and stared at the locket.

"I am not...I believe so..."

Jaclyn threw back her head and cried another anguished scream.

The guards looked at Sterling in fear.

"Lord Sterling, shall we take her—?"

"NO!" Sterling screamed. He spun around and scanned the men standing next to him. He pointed at a young member of the King's Guard. The guard swallowed hard.

"You! Boy!"

"Yes, Lord Sterling!"

"Give me your sword," Sterling snarled.

The guard nodded. He unsheathed his sword with trembling hands. Sterling snatched it away from him.

Sterling turned to the body.

He roared. He raised the sword above his head and screamed horrible words as he brought the sword down at the neck of the charred corpse.

One more strike of the blade, and the corpse's head was severed. Sterling continued to scream curses as he hacked at the body, again and again.

Lucien turned away and vomited. Many of the others did as well.

Jaclyn screamed until she lost consciousness. She hung limply against the arms of the guards. They froze in place, not knowing what to do.

Sterling stopped, at last. His heavy breathing and the continued retching of some of the guards were the only sounds to be heard.

Sterling handed the sword back to its owner.

"This will need repair."

Sterling stormed from the dungeon without

another word. Raynard and the other members of the King's Guard followed.

The guard whose sword Sterling had borrowed lingered behind until he was the last one remaining in the dungeon. He looked among the charred bodies of his fallen comrades until he found a sword in good condition. He pulled the sword free from the dead soldier's hands.

The guard took the sword that had been defiled by Lord Sterling in both of his hands.

He ground his teeth together and then cried out as he threw the sword as far into the shadows of the dungeon as he could. He sheathed the sword he had taken from the dead soldier and ran out of the dungeon.

The dungeon was silent except for the echoing of dripping water.

A sleek, jet-black wolf stepped from the shadows.

The wolf rose on its hind legs and stretched. The wolf transformed into a woman, draped in a flowing black dress.

Lady Magdalena looked around the room. She sighed.

"Will it never end?" she whispered to no one.

The woman became a wolf once again. She ran along the corridor wall and out into the night.

THIRTY-SIX

The sun was no more.

Only a few miles farther... Simon thought.

And then the first cramp hit him—at the base of his wings

Where it always began...

Simon cried out. His wings spasmed, and he fell from the sky.

Helena screamed. Simon flapped twice more before the next wave of excruciating pain washed over him.

"Hold on, Helena!" Simon cried through clenched teeth. "I have to land!"

There was no clearing in sight. Simon crashed through treetops. Helena fell for the last several feet, landing in a pile of soft, dead leaves. Simon rolled to a stop. He got to his feet, breathing hard. He arched his neck, raised his head to the sky and loosed a horrible, gut-wrenching roar. Helena tried to get to her feet. She pushed herself back against a tree trunk. Her eyes were wide.

"Oh, no, oh, no!" she whimpered. "What is happening? Simon—?"

Simon dropped his head and struggled to breathe.

"Your dress—," he panted. "Tear a piece from your dress—a piece large enough…large enough for a loincloth."

"I do not understand—"

Simon jerked his head up again and screamed. He blew a towering blast of fire that burned above the tops of the trees.

He whipped his head down and glared at Helena. His eyes filled with a desperate madness.

"DO IT!"

Helena tore at her dress with trembling fingers. She took the piece of cloth and crept toward Simon. She laid it at his feet and then hid behind a tree. When Simon screamed again, she peered out at him. She could not turn her eyes away again.

To the symphony of Simon's screams, the dragon's wings drew inward.

How can he live through such torment? Helena thought.

The dragon's scales faded away into smooth skin. The massive and terrible head shrank, smaller and smaller, until it became…

The most handsome face she had ever seen in her life.

The man sat on the ground, his shoulders heaving.

As his breathing slowed, his arms stretched out. He picked up the piece of cloth and wrapped it around his waist.

He slowly climbed to his feet, and as he turned he said,

"I'm sorry that I spoke so roughly, but—"

Helena stared at Simon. She covered her mouth with both of her hands. Tears streamed down her cheeks. She fell to her knees. Simon ran to her side.

"What is wrong Helena? Are you—?"

Helena shook her head.

"It is true! It is all true! My queen is married to the wrong man! You are the rightful King! And you are so...so...

"Oh, it is no wonder she loves—!"

"Did she say that?" Simon asked. "Did the Queen say that?"

"I have spoken out of turn," Helena whispered. "It is not my place to speak the Queen's heart."

"Our cave is perhaps two miles away. We must hurry. If I was overheard, there is no time to waste."

Simon took Helena's hand and turned to run. Helena's hand slipped from his. She stumbled and fell and cried out.

"You must keep up—"

Helena's torn dress rode up on her leg and Simon saw what was wrong.

"By the gods," Simon whispered.

Helena's leg was burned. And quite badly.

"You cannot walk?" Simon asked.

Helena pushed to her feet.

"I will try."

Helena refused to let a cry escape her lips, but she could only limp.

"I will have to carry you," Simon said. "It will not be quick, with bare feet."

Simon carried Helena at a brisk walking pace. They stopped to rest briefly. Soon after they started again, they heard rustling in the trees ahead. Simon eased Helena to the ground. He held a finger to his lips.

Helena reached inside of her dress and brought out the one thing she had carried away from the dungeon—the Queen's dagger. She handed it to Simon.

They hid behind a tree as the rustling came nearer. Simon jumped out with the dagger held high over his head.

"No, no, no, no! Simon! It's me!"

"Ah, you scared the blood out of us, Boone!" Simon exclaimed. "Gods, but I'm happy to see you!"

Boone and Simon laughed as they embraced. Boone pushed Simon away.

"Wait a minute—what do you mean, 'us'—?"

Helena had pushed herself to her feet. She leaned against the tree.

"Noooo," Boone whispered. His jaw hung slack.

Boone looked left and right. He shook his head.

"Don't tell me….do you have the queen?"

"The queen is not here," Helena said. "Only her handmaid. My name is—"

"Helena," Boone said.

"How do you know my name?" Helena leaned toward Boone. "Who are you—?"

Helena's mouth continued to work, but no words came. She looked from Boone to Simon and back again.

"It is you!" she said. "I saw you—I spoke to you—in front of the castle! I remember! You were trying to hide your faces—both of you! Pretending to be traveling merchants from across the sea!"

"You see?" Boone said to Simon. "I told you it was foolish to walk into the village. How many others know our faces now?"

"Don't turn into a nervous old woman, Boone," Simon said with a wave of his hand.

"Only two people in the world have ever seen me as dragon and man—and I'm looking at them both."

"What about the queen?" Helena asked. "She has never—?"

"No," Simon and Boone said at the same time.

"I don't suppose you brought along another pair of boots," Simon said.

"If you remember, your Grace, I haven't seen you for three nights," Boone said. "The last thing I knew, you were going out in the morning to steal from a hunt."

"He was stealing from a hunt led by the king!" Helena said. "And that is how—"

Simon blushed.

"We need to travel now, and tell tales later," he said.

"Helena cannot walk, Boone," Simon said. "One of us will have to carry her."

"What happened to you?" Boone asked.

Helena pulled up her dress to uncover her leg.

"Great Vehallion's ghost!" Boone cried. He looked at Simon.

"Did you—?"

"Do not dare say a bad thing about him!" Helena scolded. "Because of him, I am alive. The queen is alive, and the chance that this wretched curse might yet be broken is still alive, as well!"

"I was not about to—" Boone said.

"I will tell you who is not alive!" Helena continued. "Many members of the King's army—and the King's Guard! They could not stop the True King! The Dragon King!"

Boone gulped. He looked at Simon.

"Well, there you have it. You have at least three loyal subjects."

"I'll carry her," Simon said. "But, I must borrow your boots. It is too much—"

"No," Boone said. "You must be exhausted. I'll carry her."

"Well, if it's not too much trouble," Simon said with a smirk.

Boone did not look at Simon.

"No trouble."

Boone held his hand out to Helena.

"My Lady."

THIRTY-SEVEN

Boone lowered Helena to her feet at the cave's entrance.

"Here we are. Welcome to our humble home," he said.

"Our home until tomorrow tonight," Simon said. "I know we're all tired of running—but we're much too close to the village."

"You're welcome to take my bed, My Lady," Boone said. "It's only dry leaves and straw, but it's far more comfortable than the floor."

Helena put some weight on her injured leg and grimaced.

"I should walk. My leg is stiffening up—this cannot be good."

Boone struggled to find the right thing to say.

"Will you be...are you... staying with us?"

"She has nowhere else, Boone," Simon said. "Jaclyn came to the dungeon to rescue me. She was trying to open my shackles when Helena came and dragged her away. We left Helena's locket on the chest of a burned soldier. We can only hope that Sterling and the others believe she lies among the bodies that litter the dungeon floor."

Simon turned to Helena.

"If you will excuse me, I have to step outside."

Boone blew out a breath.

"I'm most grateful for your brave deeds, My Lady. But the truth is, every soldier in the realm searches for us—"

"Minus many of their best men!" Helena said.

"I'll grant you that," Boone said. "But our lives become more difficult by the hour. We move frequently, by necessity. We sleep in damp, moldy caves. Winter will soon be upon us. When winter comes, we spend many days doing nothing but hunting and shivering inside of animal skins."

Simon stepped back inside the cave. He wore a new shirt, trousers, and a new pair of boots.

Helena folded her arms.

"How difficult can your lives be—clad in new clothes?"

"These are the first new clothes I've worn since—"

"I grew up in a house full of men," Helena said. "I am not some frightened little girl—trembling at the sight of frogs and spiders. And you will need all the help you can get—unless your plan is to overthrow the Kingdom by yourself!"

"Plan?" Boone said. "What plan do you speak of?"

Helena's jaw hung slack.

"You don't…please, tell me that there is a plan. Surely, you have not hidden all of these years merely to continue to draw breath."

"I have had to survive on my own since my sixth year, M'Lady," Simon said. "Though I was on the verge of starvation when Boone saved me. He was only a boy of eleven at the time, but a skilled hunter—and braver than anyone I have ever known. Perhaps he chose to stay with me because of his own terrors—"

"Why do you lay bare our hardships?" Boone said. "Are we objects of pity—?"

"What does it serve us to hide, Boone?" Simon said. "Is this the time to hide the truth behind a wall of shame? I think not. Our friends are few, and our circle of trust is small. The time for secrets is past—if there was ever such a time at all."

"If it is truth you want to hear, then I will tell you some," Boone said. "Suppose the curse was broken, somehow. What good would that do? Do you think we could just walk the King's Road into Morgenwraithe, march up to the castle, and tell Lucien and Sterling to leave? We will need an army of some kind, your Grace."

"I know of an army," Helena said.

Simon and Boone stared at her.

"Oh, you do," Boone said. "Well, I wish we would have known about this earlier. I grow tired of sleeping on beds made of leaves."

Helena glared at Boone and then at Simon.

"Clearly, you do not choose your friends according to manners."

"Boone has manners. Sometimes," Simon said.

"Please forgive us, if we are skeptical. What army do you speak of?"

"My father and his brothers used to gather together around the fire. They either thought I could not hear, or that I would not care about the serious matters they spoke of. They spoke of forming alliances with villages in the south. They spoke of an uprising—a rebellion."

Simon ran a hand through his hair.

"I have never heard of a threat coming from the south. I always heard it said that the people of the Southlands were ignorant and backward barbarians. It is said that they barely tolerate their own neighbors, let alone present a threat to Morgenwraithe. They have few weapons and no knowledge of warfare."

"We were always told the same thing," Helena said. "But I heard different in the days before the King's army invaded our village. King Bailin made a treaty with the people of the Southlands to supply them with goods from the merchant ships. The people swore to stay south of the border and stay out of the Kingdom's affairs. But Bailin sent fewer and fewer supplies to the South. And Sterling has treated them even worse.

"The Southlanders used to receive medicine from the bounty of the merchant ships. My father said since the supplies have stopped, every time one of their people dies from sickness or disease their anger for the north grows."

"Sterling will just send the army there and destroy

them," Boone said.

"It is not that simple—not at all," Helena said. "The Southlands are surrounded by dense forests and treacherous canyons."

"My brother ran away from home twice," Boone said. "The first time he left, he traveled into the Southlands. I assume that he returned there. He told me that the only passable entry is a choke point between two mountains."

"That would discourage an invasion, even by a superior army," Simon said. "Any invading army could be surrounded and cut off from aid or supplies."

Helena sniffed.

"If only…if only we could have avoided Sterling for a little while longer. If my village and their allies could have combined forces with the true King…"

"You believe your people would have been willing to ally with a dragon?" Simon asked.

"My father, and the others in my village—they were desperate—but they were not fools. They would have listened to you," Helena said.

"He is smart," Boone said. "By far, the smartest dragon I've ever known."

"We must take the sorceress, somehow," Helena said.

"That will be most difficult," Boone said. "She is practically untouchable. Besides her magic, she is protected by Sterling and by the throne. "

"They do not protect her," Simon said. "They

protect the curse. No one knows what would happen should Magdalena die."

"Why is she loyal to Lucien? Or to Sterling?" Helena asked.

"I do not believe she is loyal at all," Simon said. "She holds the power of my curse over them. And they do not fear her because her magic is of no use against the throne."

Helena nodded slowly.

"Then her magic is also of no use against the Queen!"

"I do not know what you are saying, but I would never ask the Queen to risk—"

"To risk herself?" Helena cried. "The Queen murdered a guard to save you!"

"What?" Boone exclaimed. "The Queen murdered a guard?"

"Do you know nothing of her misery, My Lord—?"

"He is not a 'Lord', he is KING!" Boone said.

"You do not know the pain my Queen lives with! She does not love Lucien! Her only concern is her family and the people of Islemar. I live in fear that she may throw herself headlong into the sea, or put a blade into her heart like....like..."

"Like my mother did," Simon said.

"Do you think Jaclyn is safe now, Simon?" Boone asked.

"Oh, so you may call him by his given name, but if I call him 'Lord', you want to give me a spanking!" Helena cried.

"Perhaps a sound spanking would serve you well!" Boone said.

"Forgive me," Simon said. "I thought the two of you had just met, but obviously you have been married for years!"

Boone glared at Simon.

"Very fun—"

Helena swayed. Her knees buckled, and she slumped against the wall of the cave. Simon and Boone jumped to catch her but Boone was closer. Helena's dress rode up on her leg. Her wound was red and her leg was swollen.

Boone put his hand to Helena's face. He gulped and looked at Simon.

"She burns with fever. We will need—"

"Water," Simon said. "Clean water."

Simon snatched up two buckets and ran to the stream.

Boone led Helena to the corner, and his straw bed. He spread his coat and his spare shirt and helped her to lie down.

Simon returned with the water. He soaked a rag and put it on her forehead. He poured some on her wound. Helena jumped and tried to talk, but the fever made her delirious and sapped her energy.

Helena slipped into a fitful sleep.

"We are not far from the village," Boone whispered.

"I don't know what you are thinking, Boone, but I know I won't like it," Simon said.

"The apothecary is near the edge of town. We need poultice and bandages."

"So you propose that we knock on the door in the middle of the night—with every soldier in the realm looking for us. Have you lost your mind?"

"I'll go alone. And I do not intend to knock."

"In the dark," Simon said. "You would have to be lucky just to keep from breaking your neck. How will you find anything when you cannot see? I know you want to help her, Boone, but—"

"Listen to me, Simon. Her wound is bad. The fever is her body attempting to fight against infection—but she will lose that fight. My Gram died from much less of a burn than that."

Simon put his hand on Boone's shoulder.

"I know this is true. But getting yourself killed will not save her."

"No. But if I stay here and do nothing, she will die. And I will see her face every waking minute, and every night—while sleep escapes me."

"Take this," Simon said. "Perhaps it will bring you good fortune. It did for me."

"Is this the same dagger you almost killed me with earlier this evening?" Boone asked.

"The very same. It belongs to the queen."

"The queen?" Boone said. "This is the dagger she—?"

Simon nodded.

Boone slipped the dagger sheath into his belt.

"The queen's dagger," he said. "The songs that the minstrels sing of us will be rich indeed."

THIRTY-EIGHT

Boone ran down the mountainside in the faint light of the moon. He fell hard twice. The pain of a sprained ankle accompanied his every step, but did not slow him down.

He breathed heavily as he stood at the edge of the woods, staring into the silent street at the edge of the village. Three oil lamps lit the street corners. As he looked on, a lamp flickered and went out.

Boone had distant memories of the apothecary. He had been there three times he could remember — with his mother. That had been several years ago when his mother was still able to go into the village.

Boone's mother begged him not to tell his father about their visits to the healer and his shop. Boone promised that he would rather die than betray her. And it was the truth. He was well aware that she suffered from his father's regular abuse. He would gladly have taken it all upon himself to protect her. If he could not protect her, he would certainly help her to visit the healer and receive his medicine.

He was only a little boy. He could not fight. But he could keep secrets.

Another small building adjoined the apothecary. Boone squeezed his eyes shut and searched his memory.

No, it is not a shop, he thought.

The apothecary's owner—the healer and his wife—they live there.

Boone noticed the faint glow of a light or a candle behind a window. He crept around the walls of the shop and tried both doors. Locked. He pulled on windows. All locked, as well. Boone was not surprised. He went to the window furthest from the healer's residence. He took out the dagger. Slowly and quietly, he worked at opening the window. He jumped and cut his finger when he heard a dog bark in the distance.

After twenty minutes he had the window free. He pulled himself inside at a very slow pace.

Light from one of the two street lamps shone through two of the windows. Boone got on his knees and squinted to read the labels of the bottles that lined the shelves. He murmured his thanks for every painstaking moment that Simon spent teaching him the skill.

His eyes opened wide when he read a label that read,

Healing Salve. For cuts, burns—

"Make one move and I'll run you through!"

Boone froze, but not quickly enough. He jerked backward and felt a sharp pain in the middle of his back. He held up his hands.

The voice was rough, but Boone was certain it was

a woman's voice.

He sensed movement behind him and heard something strike the floor. And then something else.

"Move backward," the voice said.

Boone scooted back. There was an unlit lamp next to him. And something else that he did not recognize.

"Light the lamp," the voice said.

"How?" Boone said.

"With the striker, Idiot."

"St—striker? I do not know what that is."

"You cannot work a striker but you are certainly able to invade my shop through a locked window, you piece of filth! Do you live in a cave?"

Boone picked up the piece of metal next to the lamp.

"I'll…I'll figure it out, My Lady. I'm not stupid."

"You have a sword at your back and have committed an offense that will send you to the stocks, if not the King's dungeon. You may not know of your ignorance, but it is obvious to me."

Twenty seconds later, the lamp glowed.

"Get to your feet—holding the lamp," the woman said.

Boone stood slowly.

"Turn around—and keep your hands where I can see them. You move too fast, and I'll gut you like a fish."

"No, M'Lady."

"Save your manners, filth. It's a bit late for that."

Boone turned, with his hands held high.

"Set the lamp down," the woman said. "Let me get a look at you."

Boone recognized the woman immediately. He swallowed hard. He remembered standing in the corner of that very shop as this same woman tended to his mother. The woman spoke to his mother quietly. They always left the shop with multiple bottles.

And Boone could never recall seeing coins change hands.

The tip of the sword was now at his heart.

The old woman squinted in the lamplight.

"Put the lamp on the table. I can't see a bloody thing."

Boone sat the lamp down and raised his open hand.

"Don't I know you?" The woman leaned forward.

Boone said nothing.

The woman's eyes opened wide.

"Of course..."

The tip of the sword fell.

"They killed them—murdered them both, didn't they?"

Boone offered nothing.

"They spread the story that the dragon killed your parents and then burned down the house. The damned fools in this village choose to believe every bit of it. The story gets even better the more it's told."

The woman leaned toward Boone.

"They're even saying now that the dragon bit off their heads. Your old man deserved whatever he got, he did. And I don't give a tinker's damn what you think about that."

"He did deserve to die," Boone said. "I would have done it myself, if I was able."

The woman stared at her sword. She raised it to Boone's neck, and then she laid it on a nearby table.

"You've stood in this room more than once, with your mother. If that little boy could raise a hand against me, then my faith in humankind is lost, anyway."

"I should have killed him in his sleep," Boone said. "In his drunken stupor, I could have done it."

The old woman shook her head.

"It should never be that easy, my boy. There is justice, sure. But turning your back on family is the hardest thing a man is ever asked to do."

"You helped my mother," Boone said. "For which I shall be ever grateful. If you wish to deliver me to the King's Guard, I will understand. I will not resist."

The woman stared at Boone.

"They say you have befriended the cursed heir of Morgenwraithe. Is this true?"

"It is."

"My husband is away—he sailed on a merchant's vessel because we've learned about new medicines available across the sea. That is the reason you are still alive, young Mister Blankenship. The corridor between our home and this shop remains open—and lined with snares. My husband sleeps with a loaded crossbow within two paces of our bed."

"I understand, My Lady," Boone said.

"The throne has been a poison upon our people since I was a little girl," the woman said.

"I believe it has, My Lady," Boone said.

The woman leaned forward. She grabbed Boone by his shoulders.

"The true heir of Morgenwraithe. Tell me.

"Tell me he is a good man."

"He is the best man I have ever known, My Lady. I swear it upon my mother's life."

The woman lowered her hands.

"Is he hurt badly?"

"The medicine we need is not for him, My Lady. It is for—"

"Ah, ah, ah! I do not want to know!"

The woman packed a sack with several poultices, bandages, and salve. She added bread and meat.

"Thank you, My Lady," Boone said. "I will not darken your doorway again."

"Wait," the woman said.

She stepped forward and stared into Boone's face for a moment. The woman walked to a rack of shawls and took one down. She put it back, and took down another that was lined with lace. She handed it to Boone.

Boone took the shawl and put it into the sack.

"How did you know?" Boone asked.

"Believe it or not, I was a young girl once," the woman smiled. "And young girls become very good at reading the faces of young men."

"Thank you," Boone said. "I wish you well."

"Take care of the girl. And take care of...him. I wish us all well."

THIRTY-NINE

Simon checked on Helena. She continued to sleep, with intermittent moans and words he could not comprehend. Beads of sweat dotted her face despite the cool air inside the cave. Simon soaked the rag in the chilled water and placed it on her forehead.

He stepped outside and stared down the mountainside the darkness toward the village.

His friend had been gone for hours—on a dangerously impossible mission.

While his newest friend struggled to stay alive.

Simon thought he heard noises below, crashing through the brush. He prayed that it was Boone. He was without weapons and helpless.

If it was enemies that approached, his life would soon be over.

"Simon! It's me! I'm back!"

Boone and Simon treated Helena's wound and then collapsed to the floor.

"You amaze me again, my friend," Simon said.

"Don't be so quick to make me out the hero. Not long ago, I had the tip of a sword at my back. I could have died by the hand of an old woman."

"You didn't..."

"Kill her?" Boone said. "No. The woman knew me. She remembered my mother."

"Then both you and Helena may be saved—by a miracle," Simon said.

"It was far more than a miracle, Your Grace. I am beginning to believe that the heart of a resistance beats inside of the realm. If I dare say it—I actually believe they would unite behind you. They seek a better destiny than what lies before them."

"The people united—behind the dragon," Simon said. "The minstrels will certainly never suffer for new tales to sing."

"Aye!" Boone said.

"I am thirsty," Helena said. Simon and Boone leaped to their feet.

"I cannot thank you enough," Helena said.

Simon held his hand toward Boone.

"You can thank Lord Blankenship—whose madness knows no bounds. A brave soul is he—a man whose head and heart do not know the meaning of the word 'impossible'."

"That was beautiful," Boone said. "Write that down for me—while you still have hands."

Helena put a hand to her mouth.

"I had completely forgotten. You have wasted much of the full moon day to help me."

"A waste?" Boone said. "I think not. You represent one-third of the new Kingdom."

"I beg to argue, Lord Blankenship," Helena said. "One-fourth."

"Who do you include?" Simon asked.

"The Queen, of course."

They paused in awkward silence.

"You return to—to your other body, at the next moon?" Helena asked.

"Yes," Simon said.

"Is it as terrible—as before?"

"No, no, no! Nothing like that."

"I think he enjoys it, myself," Boone smirked.

"I must admit," Simon said. "The transformation is most pleasurable—which makes it far worse."

"Worse? Why?" Helena asked.

"The pleasure works against the will. I am always aware of it—every day. The memory fights against my will to break the curse. Some part of me fights to keep the dragon alive."

"I believe this fight makes you stronger, Your Grace," Helena said.

Boone nodded in agreement.

"We shall see," Simon said.

Helena's eyelids fluttered. Boone jumped to her side.

"Lie back down, My Lady. Oh, I almost forgot."

Boone grabbed the sack he had carried from the apothecary. He took out the shawl, and put it around Helena's shoulders.

"Where did you get this?" she said.

"It was a gift—from a friend."

"We should move soon," Boone said.

"Yes," Simon said. "I was thinking—"

"Do you have sanctuaries near the Southland borders?" Helena asked.

"Yes, there are two," Simon said.

"We should go there," Helena said. "We should scout the Southlands—while the bonds formed by my father and his brothers are still remembered."

Boone shook his head.

"Our immediate concern should be to see that you return to good health. I believe we should take refuge near Islemar. The salt air will be good for you."

"I must agree with Boone, My Lady," Simon said. "At least for a short time. Sterling is not likely to send his armies into Islemar. Lord Lamont is likely the only man in the realm that Sterling truly fears."

"There is wisdom in going to Islemar," Helena said. "If your intent is to keep hiding. You will raise no army there."

Simon stared at Helena.

"We will travel to the Southlands—when we are all strong enough," he said.

"That is how things work in the new Kingdom, My Lady," Boone said. "Fair and square. Two votes to one."

Simon walked away from the cave before sunset. He took to the air and flew over the route he would take later, with Boone and Helena on his back. He dropped down near the chosen cave that stood high above the sea. There was a constant breeze. There were no signs of human presence there since the last time he used it.

When the three landed there later that night, Boone helped Helen from Simon's back.

"Well, how did you like the ride?" Boone asked.

"That was incredible!" she said. "I...I am almost ashamed. I should not take such pleasure in the King's curse."

"Do not worry," Boone said. "You heard him. There are parts he likes, as well."

Helena grew stronger in the next days. Her wound healed at an exceptional rate, aided by the salt winds.

"It is time to change the dressing, My Lady," Boone said. "We have enough for three more at best."

Helena smiled. She pulled up the tattered end of her dress.

"Then you have but three more opportunities to enjoy this view, My Lord."

Boone smiled, as well. He sighed.

"And I shall savor every one, My Lady."

FORTY

Boone hunted by day, and Simon by night.

Simon woke one day to the mouth-watering aroma of roasted fish.

"What is this delightful dish?" he asked, as he exited the cave.

Boone looked at Helena and moaned.

"I knew we should have built the fire farther away! The cove beneath us is full of these fish, Simon. But we only have twenty. You could probably eat a thousand!"

Simon looked toward the sea.

"In the cove, eh? Don't worry about me. Enjoy your meal. I will have a go at catching these fish for myself!"

Simon took flight and descended upon the cove. He discovered that he was far more adept at fishing than hunting. His vision worked exceptionally well at night. He found that he could spot schools of fish beneath the surface from the air, as well.

Helena grew tired of wood gathering and cooking. She pestered Boone enough that he began taking her on hunts. She was a tentative student of the skill.

Along with hunting, they passed their time learning reading and writing skills from Simon. Boone and Helena took turns turning the pages of books that Simon had "collected".

They built fires only when they had to. When the nights grew cold, they huddled together beneath all the clothing they had. Winter was not far away, especially in the mountains. The benefits of the healing salt winds had about run their course.

Boone and Helena left the cave at dawn.

"If we find something early, I'll track and let you have the bow. The practice has served you well—you've taken to it quickly."

"For a girl, is what you mean!" Helena teased.

"Believe me, Helena," Boone smiled. "When it comes to hunting—or combat—all I care about is skill. Not what parts the bowman carries beneath his knickers."

Helena stopped.

"What is it?" Boone said.

Helena smiled.

"You said my name."

Boone shrugged.

"Sorry, My L—"

"No," Helena said. "I liked it. I liked it very much."

"Boone."

"I liked it very much, Boone."

"Drop the bow."

Boone and Helena froze. The voice came from the trees.

Boone raised the bow instead.

"That's a poor job of dropping a bow."

That voice came from their opposite side. They were surrounded.

Boone dropped the bow and pulled Helena to his side.

Two soldiers stepped into the clearing. They sheathed their swords.

"We're looking for two men. Who is this girl?" One of the soldiers asked.

"It's not two men we seek, Lieutenant," the other said. "It's one man and a dragon!"

"Yeah, that's right," the lieutenant said. "A smart-as-a-whip talking dragon, at that!"

"Would have made a right-respectable King, don't ya think?" the second soldier said.

"Better than the sorry lot we got at Morgenwraithe now, without a doubt," the lieutenant said.

"Who are you?" Boone asked. "And how do you know so much about the...the dragon?"

The lieutenant wiped his gloves together.

"Let's just say we've met."

"Why should we believe you?" Boone asked.

"Because Lord Lamont sent us here. Actually, he sent pairs of us—six men he trusts—to three different caves nearby. We're the lucky ones who found you."

"So, you've found us. For what purpose?" Boone asked.

"Lord Lamont wishes to speak to you and...your large friend. He will come here within three days."

"Very well," Boone said. "He will be welcome. Please, tell Lord Lamont to signal his arrival. Dragons can be...unpredictable."

The soldiers laughed. They turned to leave.

"Oh. I almost forgot," the lieutenant said.

He stepped into the trees and returned with a bundle.

"Blankets. Lady Lamont's idea. It gets cold up here."

"That it does," Boone said. "Thank you."

"Yes, Thank you, very much," Helena said.

"I don't know who you are, Miss, but your friends have a difficult life ahead of them," the lieutenant said.

"I am where I am meant to be," Helena said.

"We wish you well," the soldiers bowed their heads, and walked away.

"This is destiny at work," Simon said. "I have believed for some time, that if I am to retake the throne, Islemar and Lord Lamont will play a role."

"A role of support, perhaps," Helena said. "But

they haven't enough numbers to—"

"Numbers are important," Simon said. "But more important still, are brave leaders who people are willing to follow. Lord Lamont is such a man."

Two days later, their studies were interrupted. "You there! Lord Lamont desires an audience!"

"Well, speak of the devil," Boone said. Simon and Helena glared at him. "Just a figure of speech."

Lord Lamont and his lieutenant entered the cave. "Welcome to Islemar," he said. He rubbed his hands together.

"Winter has come early."

"That it has, Lord Lamont," Simon said. "Thank you for the blankets."

"Do you feel the cold, by the way?" Lamont asked.

"Not when I fly, or move about," Simon said. "As long as I have food in my belly, the cold does not reach me."

Lamont nodded.

"We have been to visit the Queen," he said. "Robin and…I dare say, Lady Lamont and I."

"How is she, My Lord?" Helena asked.

Lamont had not noticed Helena.

"Do I—are you Jaclyn's handmaid?"

"Yes, My Lord."

"By the gods!" Lamont exclaimed. "She thinks you

are dead! She will be so happy—!"

"She cannot know, Lord Lamont," Simon said softly. "Not yet."

"She would never tell anyone," Lamont said. "I would swear that on my life!"

"It is safer for the Queen if she does not know," Simon said. "It is also safer for Helena and for Boone and me. It is dangerous to arouse Sterling's suspicions."

Lamont slammed his fist into his hand.

"I lie awake and dream of separating that devil's head from his shoulders. He has been nothing but poison to this Realm!"

"We are of one accord on this matter, Lord Lamont," Boone said.

Lamont blew out a long breath.

"You are right, of course. It is just that the thought of being able to take Jaclyn a piece of good news is intoxicating to me now. The Queen...my Jaclyn...she has become distant. Forlorn. Depressed beyond measure. She does not sleep.

"I thought I had given her the greatest gift of all—the throne of Morgenwraithe. She was forever at my side—a delight."

Lamont chuckled.

"She was never what you would call—'ladylike'. I'm to blame for that. My little girl has become queen—and my heart breaks at what has become of her."

"Lord Lamont," Simon said. "The curse that protects the throne against magic—does it extend to the

King's Regent?"

Lamont sighed.

"There is no way to know. It has never been tested."

"What about poison?" Boone asked. "If it did not work, he would be none the wiser in the effort."

"Sterling has tasters—at least two young boys," Helena said. "They follow him everywhere and test every drop and morsel that goes into his mouth. I have seen the boys so drunk they cannot stand."

"The curse of protection on the throne is not the curse we should be concerned with," Lamont said. "If Magdalena's spell is broken, the people will follow us. I know this as sure as I am standing before you. It will require bloodshed, but the people hunger for a better life.

"They need a champion to lead them. The redemption of the rightful king will give them their noble purpose."

"We have spoken of traveling to the Southlands," Simon said. "Helena's people were preparing alliances there when Sterling sensed the beginnings of rebellion. We know what followed."

"Aye, the slaughter of an entire village of good and innocent people," Lamont said. "I met your father, Helena. And his brothers. I sensed that they were up to something—but they never mentioned it to me.

"We should be going. I will think on what you have said about the Southlands. And we should all think hard on how we might lay hold of the sorceress. At the edge of the clearing, due south, you will find a little gift."

"You are too kind, Lord Lamont," Simon said.

"It is nothing, really. Four fat goats."

Lamont reached his hand toward Simon. Simon stiffened.

Lamont laughed and patted Simon's belly.

"We will need plenty of fire in the days to come, Your Grace."

"It will be my honor, Viceroy Lamont."

"Let us see I never have to exercise that title, shall we?"

"Agreed."

"You should have a signal—for when you return here, Lord Lamont," Boone said. "My large friend, here, he does not respond well to surprise."

Lamont stroked his beard.

"What about...All hail the true King!"

FORTY-ONE

Helena became more skilled with a bow, learning at Boone's side. Simon visited the cove twice a day. One dive into the frigid waters never failed to provide him less than a full catch. He carried the fish to the mouth of the cave where he roasted them with one blast from his jaws.

Fishing did not bother Simon as much as having to look into the frightened eyes of animals. Although winter was upon them, no one would starve.

Three days later, they heard a voice from below them on the mountainside.

"All hail, the true King!"

"We did not expect to see you so soon, Lord Lamont," Simon said.

Lamont wore a serious expression.

"The queen is with child."

Simon sat down hard on the forest floor.

"What does this mean—for the realm?" Boone asked.

"If it is a boy child, it means that the line of kings is secure, and Sterling has nothing to fear from my position as Viceroy," Lamont said. "That is a good thing. We will have the freedom to seek support in the Southlands without drawing his attention."

"You are forgetting one possibility," Simon said.

"What?" Boone said.

"Sterling holds the position of regent until Lucien's seventeenth name day," Simon said.

"That is the law," Lamont said.

"By the gods!" Helena said. "Could Sterling be so evil—?"

"What are you talking about?" Boone asked.

"If it would cross the mind of any man, it would be Lord Sterling," Lamont said.

Boone shrugged. He was puzzled.

"If Lucien and Jaclyn have a boy child," Helena said. "Sterling could remain Regent for seventeen more years."

"That is not possible," Boone said. "The only way that could happen is if—"

Realization came over Boone's face.

"He wouldn't! Murder Lucien? Simon? What hellish spirit does Sterling possess?"

"I will see this madness come to an end, if I have to raze the castle to the ground," Simon said. "I would begin tonight, if I knew I could put an end to this terror."

"Jaclyn is in even more danger than the King," Lamont said. "I have just come from Morgenwraithe.

Lady Lamont remains there. I have seen the faces of both Lucien and Sterling. They are sorely displeased with Jaclyn's reaction to the child."

Lord Lamont's voice broke. "Forgive me. Seeing her so unhappy was already hard to bear. To see her miserable at the thought of having her first child…it is not only painful for me to see. It is making the King and his Regent most angry. And there is nothing I or my wife can do."

"If you will excuse me, Lord Lamont," Simon said. "I need…a few moments."

Lamont nodded. Simon stepped out of the cave. He took to the air. The others paused in the silence of their thoughts.

Their heads jerked up when they heard an awful roar echo against the mountains.

Lord Lamont, his lieutenant, Boone, and Helena studied each other's faces.

"He is a passionate dragon," Lamont said.

"He is also a passionate man," Helena said.

"Aye," Boone said.

"You have seen him, then—in his human form?" Lamont asked.

"Yes," Helena said.

"Has the Queen—?"

"No," Boone and Helena said together.

"This passion will be needed in the days to come—as well as his strength and fire—"

"He loves her, Lord Lamont," Helena said. "And she loves him."

The lieutenant looked clearly uncomfortable. He stepped outside of the cave.

Lamont stroked his beard. He flexed his hands and stared at the wall.

"I feared as much," he whispered.

"Nothing. Nothing in my life could have prepared me for what we face."

"I have not lived many years, My Lord," Boone said. "But I have lived long enough to see good, and to know evil. We may all perish in the fight. But we must fight. Or evil will consume us all."

"It is that simple, is it not?" Lamont smiled. "Who would have thought such wisdom could come from such a young mind? We must ensure you and your friends have a proper world in which to grow old."

"We will need an army," Helena said.

"And an army we shall have!" Lamont said.

There was a rustling in the trees as Simon made his way back to the cave entrance.

"I must be off," Lamont said. "I hate leaving my wife and daughter alone in that place. Concerning the Southlands —,"

"We must move soon, Lord Lamont," Simon said. "Sterling and his spies will be on full alert now. It is dangerous for us to remain so close to Islemar — and dangerous for you."

"But what about plans for the Southlands?" Helena asked. "How much time do we have left to act? Do we wait for Sterling to force our hands?"

"It will take weeks to raise support in the south, at best. And if Lord Lamont and his officers are not known to be either in Islemar or Morgenwraithe, it will arouse Sterling's suspicion," Simon said. "There is one thing of immediate importance to our cause," Simon said.

"What is that?" Lamont asked.

"We must convince the queen to alter her behavior. To put forth a convincing act."

Lamont dropped his chin to his chest.

"Have you not heard me, Simon?" Lamont asked. "You ask the impossible. She has no hope—"

"Then we must give her hope!" Simon said.

"How do we accomplish that?" Boone asked.

"I have given this more thought. We should inform her of our plans," Simon said. "And tell her that Helena is alive and well."

"You've done quite a turnabout on that fact," Boone said.

"Yes, I have," Simon said. "But our cause grows more desperate. If the queen continues in misery and sorrow, the castle will be full of whispers. This will not escape Sterling's attention. And should the queen deliver an heir—

"Then many lives are in danger."

"This is true," Lamont said. "I will go to

Morgenwraithe immediately. I will secure a private
audience with Jaclyn—"

"No," Simon said.

"No?" Lamont, Boone, and Helena said together.

"If I know Lord Sterling at all," Simon said, "there
will be nowhere inside of the castle you or Lady Lamont
can exchange a private word. This will be especially true,
now."

"Then what do you propose?" Lamont asked.

"The full moon will be upon us in one week."

"What?" Boone exclaimed. "What are you
thinking, Simon? Or are you thinking at all!"

Helena tugged at Boone's sleeve.

"Boone. You are yelling at the King!"

Boone yanked his arm away.

"I am aware of that, my Lady! And I am duty-
bound to see that the king remains alive! But it sounds as
if he seeks to throw his life down a privy-hole!"

"What I propose is less dangerous than asking
Lord Lamont to risk himself, his wife, his daughter, and
his entire village!"

"What you propose—is foolish!" Boone yelled.

"It is not foolish!" Simon said.

Boone waved his hands and paced.

"Ain't love just grand, Your Grace? Winks and
giggles! Hearts all a-flutter! Flowery words sung by
minstrels—"

"Hold your tongue!" the dragon roared. Helena

and Lamont stepped back.

Boone stomped across the floor and stood in front of Simon. He clenched his fists.

"I will not hold my tongue! You are not the first man—the first dragon—to be in love! But I will be damned if I will be silent while it kills you!"

Several moments of silence passed.

"I know you speak from a place of friendship, and from passion," Simon said. "And for that, I am grateful."

"Lord Lamont."

"Yes?" Lamont said.

"Can you be at Morgenwraithe on the day of the full moon?"

"I can."

"Press a note into Jaclyn's hand. Make it say, 'Light a candle at midnight where you last met a friend'."

FORTY-TWO

Jaclyn sat in her chair, staring out of the window at an afternoon dark with rain.

She was startled when she heard a voice. She heard no one enter the room.

"Ah, another lovely day at Morgenwraithe. It matches the mood, as always, wouldn't you say?"

Jaclyn turned and glared at Lady Magdalena with swollen, bloodshot eyes.

"Have you come to the King's chamber to make sport of me, Sorceress?" Jaclyn said. "It must be quite thrilling to know that in any other Kingdom you would be put to death for your words."

"Perhaps you have not noticed, but I am your visitor, and you have not offered me a seat. Has your foul demeanor destroyed your manners? Or had you ever acquired any?"

"What?" Jaclyn gripped the arms of her chair. "What did you—how dare you—!"

Magdalena laughed. She leaned against the windowsill.

"Oh, my! I have poked the Queen with a stick, and it turns out she is still alive!"

Jaclyn pushed herself to her feet.

"I will have you—!"

Magdalena lifted her hand and flipped her fingers. Jaclyn was thrown back into her chair.

"No, my Queen. What you will do, is listen to what I have to say."

"Mother!" Jaclyn said. She looked around the room.

"Where is my mother?"

Magdalena sighed.

"She may be touring the dungeon—or perhaps watching the kitchen staff butcher a boar for tonight's dinner. Either of these would be less depressing than staying another minute in this room."

"What do you want?" Jaclyn snapped.

"I want you to stop acting like a spoiled child—"

"Why do you care what I—?"

Magdalena grabbed the arms of Jaclyn's chair and leaned close to her face. She ground her teeth.

"I want you to stay alive!"

"What is that supposed to mean?" Jaclyn asked.

Magdalena pushed away from the chair.

"Do you think your behavior is endearing you to the king? Or Lord Sterling?"

"What right do you have to question my behavior?" Jaclyn asked. "You are the one to blame for this! You and your stupid curse!"

"That stupid curse put you at the right hand of the King."

"And where did it leave you, WITCH?" Jaclyn screamed.

A voice came from the hallway.

"Are you all right, My Queen?"

"Leave us!" Magdalena said sharply.

She raised her hand, and the door slammed shut.

Jaclyn gripped the chair. She breathed heavily.

"You remain untouched. You have no need to fear anyone in the Kingdom. Sterling cannot harm you. And Lucien does not dare."

Jaclyn sneered.

"You have no one to fear but the dragon."

Magdalena dragged her fingers along the windowsill.

"Of course," she purred. "I hold the only key that locks him inside of that beast, and you think I fear him? Such is the power of the dragon, my Queen! Their legend has so filled the minds of the people that death by dragon-fire is a fate worse than death itself! But, you see, this dragon has a mind—"

Jaclyn laughed.

"Yes! Yes, Sorceress. Keep telling yourself that you are dealing with a rational mind! Tell that to yourself as you burn! My handmaid—whatever her motivation was—threw her life away to save the dragon—

"What did it get her? What did her sacrifice attain?

The most horrible of deaths!"

"They will assign you a new handmaid soon,"
Magdalena said. "Do not fool yourself, my Queen. They
were well-aware that you were close to Helena. You
must not trust—"
Helena laughed again.
"Trust? Do you really expect me to listen to you
when it comes to the issue of trust?"
Magdalena stepped toward Jaclyn.
"Have you given up?"
Jaclyn was perplexed.
"What…what type of question is that?"
"Have you given up? Have you no hope—that this
life will ever be more than it is?"

Jaclyn scowled.
"Why should I stand here and listen to a lecture
from the Witch who cheated the realm? The Witch who
chose to twist the fate of the entire kingdom?"
Magdalena grabbed Jaclyn's hand. Jaclyn tried to
get away, but there was magic at work.
"Be still!" Magdalena said. Magdalena raised her
other hand.
Jaclyn continued to struggle.
"What are you doing?"
Magdalena placed her hand on Jaclyn's belly. And
then she let go.

Magdalena sighed.
"I find it difficult to imagine that even a brief

moment of passion brought this about."

"There has never been a single moment of passion—for either of us!" Jaclyn said. "Only the fulfillment of duty! Of expectation! And the fear of—!"

"The fear of Lord Sterling's wrath!" Magdalena finished.

Jaclyn's silence confirmed the truth.

Magdalena pointed at Jaclyn's belly.

"We have precious little time," Magdalena said quietly. "Our fate will be sealed when the child comes."

"What are you talking about?" Jaclyn asked.

"Climb out of your selfishness long enough to think, my Queen. The moment that Lucien has an heir, Sterling's existence as King's Regent gains new breath."

"He has but two years—" Jaclyn said.

"He has but two years if Lucien is alive!"

"You think that Sterling would kill—?"

"Lower your voice!" Magdalena whispered.

"A newborn King would afford Sterling another generation of rule—likely more ruthless than what we have already seen. And your life—"

"He will kill me, as well," Jaclyn said.

"Yes," Magdalena said. "And me."

Jaclyn looked up.

"You?"

"Yes."

"This could all be for naught," Jaclyn said. "The baby could be a girl, and—"

Magdalena shook her head.

"No."

Jaclyn put her hand to her mouth. She stared out of the window. Her shoulders fell.

Magdalena stepped beside her.

"With the birth of Lucien's heir, Simon's claim to the throne will become unclear, even if the curse was broken."

"Do you think I care?" Jaclyn asked. "If you thought to put an end to your madness, you have waited too long! He killed the girl that saved him! Whatever mind he once possessed—it is gone! He is no longer a man! The dragon has consumed him!"

Magdalena leaned close to Jaclyn's ear.

"What if I told you that your handmaid is alive?"

"You heartless, lying bit—!" Jaclyn growled as she pushed Magdalena away from her. She drew back her fist and swung at Magdalena's chin.

Magdalena leaned back at the last second. Jaclyn twirled herself around and fell to the floor. Magdalena grabbed Jaclyn's arms and pulled her to her feet with an inhuman strength.

"Liar! You are a lying witch!" Jaclyn struggled. "I saw her with my own—!"

Magdalena covered Jaclyn's mouth with her hand.

"What you saw, was not intended for your eyes. What you saw, was what was intended for Sterling to see."

Jaclyn slumped into her chair. She sobbed as she

chewed at her finger.

"Why did you come here?" Jaclyn asked. "Why did you not just let me die? You expect me to have hope—hope based on your words? I would not only have to believe Helena was alive—but that a noble heart still beats inside of that beast."

"What if I told you the dragon was dead?"

Jaclyn leaped to her feet.

"No! You are lying! Again!"

"Not a lie, my Queen," Magdalena said. "A test."

Magdalena narrowed her eyes.

"The dragon lives—somewhere within the realm. Just as he lives in your heart!"

Jaclyn glared.

"I should have you killed this instant."

"But you will not. Because I speak the truth. I am leaving now. If we are to survive, we will need for you to stop incurring the wrath and the attention of Lord Sterling. We will also need the power and fire of the one who holds the Queen's heart."

"You are truly mad—" Jaclyn said.

Magdalena dismissed herself with a wave of her hand.

"From the lips of the one in love with the dragon-King."

FORTY-THREE

Simon flew them to the sight of the cave that would become their newest temporary home. Boone slid down and helped Helena off of Simon's back.

"This cave is closer to the village than any of the others," Boone shook his head. "Is this the wisest course of action?'

"It is the last thing they would expect after my escape," Simon said.

Boone walked into the cave, looked around, and walked back out.

"They've found it, Simon!" Boone exclaimed. "The cave is stripped clean! They know we were here!"

"Just as I said before," Simon said. "They will never expect us to remain here."

"You are not thinking clearly, Simon," Boone said. "They have enough resources to investigate every possibility. They may think we would abandon this location, but that does not prevent sending someone—anyone—to have a look. It wouldn't have to be a soldier—it could be a child! What does Sterling care if you burn a child alive?"

"Your thoughts frighten me at times, Boone."

"Someone has to remain grounded in reality, Your Grace," Boone said. "Of late, I believe that responsibility has fallen to me."

"I will not argue with you."

"I will gather our beds," Helena said. "I could sleep for days."

"It will be dawn soon," Boone said. "I know this area. There should be game nearby. I will see that we have meat before I sleep."

"I will go with you," Helena said.

Boone shook his head.

"We should be extra careful while we are here. Plenty of game means a greater possibility that someone else may hunt nearby. There's a greater risk of being seen."

"Maybe you're just getting tired of having me along," Helena said.

"Don't start in with your games," Boone snapped. "We're all tired. I wish to stay alive long enough to eat and then sleep for three days."

Boone turned and started into the woods. Helena stomped her foot and snatched up her bow.

"No, Helena," Simon said. "Boone is right. He did not dismiss you. He means to keep you safe."

"He means to become my father!"

Simon chuckled.

"No, no, no. He does not mean to become your father. Make your bed and get some sleep. We will all think clearer after we have rested. We will have to."

"You are one to talk!" Helena said as she stormed away. She tossed her head and murmured out loud.

"Don't go in the woods, little girl! It's far too dangerous, little girl! But I am a dragon, and I will waltz right into the castle and visit the Queen if I wish!"

Simon lay on the floor and closed his eyes. Helena gathered the leaves and straw that littered the cave floor. She lay down, closed her eyes, and immediately began sneezing. She sneezed several times and then closed her eyes again.

Seconds later, the sneezing began again. Helena jumped to her feet in a huff. She swore as she kicked the bedding away from her. A cloud of dust rose from it. Helena stomped across the floor, and out the door.

Helena screamed.

Simon leaped to his feet and ran outside.

Helena stood still—face-to-face with a black wolf.

"Do not move," Simon whispered. He inhaled. And then he held his breath.

The wolf stood on its back legs and transformed into a tall lady in a black gown.

Magdalena grabbed Helena and stood behind her.

Helena jerked her arms. She kicked back with her feet.

Magdalena did not seem to even notice.

"What are you doing here?" Simon snarled. "Let her go!"

"Turn off your fire, and I will let her go,"
Magdalena said. "That is only fair."

"The only way to turn off the fire is to starve
myself," Simon said. "Unless you know of another way.
You are my Creator, after all."

"It was a joke, Your Highness," Magdalena said.
"It is one reason I always look forward to our meetings. I
so seldom get to express humor while in the village."

"This gives me an idea for what to do with you,"
Simon said. "We could place you in stocks, in the village
square, and let you entertain the people until your
tongue falls off."

Magdalena laughed.

"That was delicious, Dragon-King! It is a shame
that such a creative mind wastes away in filthy caves!"

"We have played these word games before,"
Simon said. "This gets us nowhere."

"No. It does not."

Magdalena lowered her hands. Helena could not
believe it. Neither could Simon.

Helena ran and hid behind the dragon.

"What is this?" Simon asked. "Some new kind of
magic?"

"No," Magdalena said. "No magic, at all. I
propose that we come together in common purpose—

"Before it is too late."

"Do not listen to the Witch!" Helena snapped.
"There is even more treachery in her truth than in her

lies! She thinks only of herself! Bring your fire and send
her to Valhalla!"

Magdalena waved her hand.

"Please, let us hear all of your insults and wishes
for my eternal damnation now, so we may get on with
the things that matter!"

"Helena has as many reasons—" Simon began.

"I know all about the Queen's handmaid,"
Magdalena said. "I attend the castle often, if that fact has
slipped your mind. Do you think it has escaped Sterling's
notice that the Queen confided in this girl much more
than she should—?"

Simon raised his head into the air and blew fire
from his nostrils.

"I will not stand silent while you insult the Queen!
Do you begrudge her having a single confidant? One
friend—in the entire Kingdom? Sterling would find a
reason to hate the Queen, even if there was no reason.
And by Helena's association with her, she is hated, as
well."

"She will tell them I am alive!" Helena said.
"Lucien and Sterling will believe that the queen was
involved in—!"

Magdalena clapped her hands and laughed.

"She is a bright child! Perhaps she will not be as
much of a liability to us as I previously thought."

"Stop talking like we are on the same side,
Sorceress!" Helena screamed. "Sim—your Grace, please
tell me that you are not listening to—"

"I could burn her to ash in seconds," Simon said softly.

"Yes, you could," Magdalena replied.

"Your Grace….Simon," Helena whispered. "NO! She is tricking you! You cannot listen to her!"

"The proof is simple," Simon said.

"Lift the curse."

FORTY-FOUR

"That is not what you want," Magdalena said. "Not now."

"Are you mad?" Simon roared.

He turned his head aside just in time. Flames blasted through the door of the cave.

"Get out, Witch. Before I lose all patience."

"You must listen to me—" Magdalena said.

"I said get out! A dragon will not sit the throne of Morgenwraithe! You dare come here to propose an alliance. To what end? Even desperate people must have someone to rally behind. Without a rightful King, there is no such man!"

"You are wrong, Simon," Magdalena said. "The people do not look for a king. They look for strength."

"Ha!" Simon said. "Did the people cheer the strength of the dragon on the king's name day? Was the arena alive with support for the mighty fire-breathing beast? Or did they curse it in the name of every burned man, woman, and child ever consumed by dragon's fire? Did they curse it for every destroyed field? The people have no love for any dragon—!"

Magdalena stared at the ground.

"It would be far too dangerous for me to attempt to lift the curse."

"I swear on all that is holy that you will not be harmed," Simon said. "I do not seek vengeance. That is not why—"

"Listen to me!" Magdalena yelled.

There was silence.

"Yes, I was born with gifts," Magdalena said quietly. "And I learned much from my Gram—but her skills were limited. Magic among women is not encouraged in the Southlands—and it is far worse within the Kingdom. The few old men with the power of magic guard their secrets. They have been watched closely since the days of Vehaillion, and they live in fear."

"Fear of what?" Simon asked.

"Fear of death!" Magdalena exclaimed. "Men who rule by fear do not trust magic! And they do not sit by and watch its secrets shared freely."

"What are you saying?" Boone said. "You cannot lift the curse? You dare come here on bended knee with no ability to—?"

"I am saying that it would present a risk!" Magdalena said.

"The old man who taught me in secret is long dead. If I tried to lift the curse, it might work. Or it may bind you inside the dragon for all eternity.

"It might even kill you."

"Then we search among those with magic who remain," Helena said. "That they may guide you."

"There are no more," Magdalena said.

Boone shook his head.

"Surely there must be someone—"

"Lord Sterling has killed them all," Magdalena said. She looked at Simon.

"The only hope for you, or for the entire kingdom—lies elsewhere."

"She is lying," Boone said. "We have seen her magic at work. She knows your curse keeps her alive."

"You are a powerful and intelligent dragon," Magdalena said. "Without the curse, you are nothing but another man."

"A man who is the rightful King!" Helena screamed. "The people know this is true!"

"I am not talking about these people."

"What are you saying?" Helena asked.

"We must raise an army in the south."

Helena and Simon exchanged a look.

"Very well, then," Simon said.

"No!" Helena shouted.

"Lift the curse, this minute," Simon said, "and we will leave for the Southlands immediately. It should be a simple campaign. How could any rational people oppose it? I have prepared my plea—listen to me, Sorceress, and tell me that I am wrong!

"I, the Dragon-King,

"Simon Morgenwraithe, the rightful King of the
land, come to you with a request of mutual benefit. Rally
your forces behind me and we will overthrow the
usurpers! We will vanquish the unjust who have kept
you poor and sick! And your reward will be gold, and
lands, access to the ports of Islemar and seats of influence
within the Kingdom!"

Magdalena shook her head.
"The people of the Southlands do not care about
'rightful kings'—or any king at all."
"How do you profess to know so much about the
Southlands?" Helena asked.
"I was born there," Magdalena said.
"You were not!" Helena said. "She's lying!"
"Why would I lie about such a thing?" Magdalena
snapped.
"Because you are a wit—!"

Magdalena's face lengthened and her mouth grew
large. An intense growl sounded behind a row of vicious
fangs.
Helena whimpered and fell silent. She stepped
back. Magdalena's face returned to normal.
Simon and Helena stared at Magdalena as she
paced the floor.
"I lived in the Southlands with my family, for
seven years. My mother took ill and died. I spent most of
my days with my Gram. We shared the power of

magic—but she warned me to keep it secret, always. I never knew why. She grew feeble and old.

"My father had a difficult time feeding us. The crops failed for three years. My brothers disappeared—one at a time. I believe they were sold, but Father would not speak of it. One day a big, gruff man came to our home. He and my father argued. They argued over the price for me. I watched the man pull a dagger and cut my father's throat.

"I ran to my Gram's hut. The man chased me there and knocked down the door. Gram ran at the man with an ax. He...he killed her. And he dragged me away with him. He brought me to Morgenwraithe and sold me the next day.

"He had me bound, hand and foot. You may think this would discourage anyone from my purchase, but it does not work that way. These people know there is far more magic in the south than in the villages of the kingdom. And many believe magic can bring them riches.

"There were many bidders. Your grandfather was chief among them."

Helena held her hand over her mouth.

"I spoke to the queen," Magdalena said.

"You spoke to her? Concerning what?" Simon asked.

"Her behavior," Magdalena said.

Simon started to object. Magdalena held up her hands.

"Her pouting behavior that threatens our purpose

and endangers her life! She has been in the throes of such depression that it is an embarrassment for Lucien and Sterling. This cannot be allowed to continue.

"I also…implied that Helena was alive."

"You…" Helena whispered. "Did you really do that?"

"We will discuss this matter," Simon said, "among ourselves."

"There is not much time," Magdalena said. "The new heir to the throne will be born in six months."

"If the child is a boy," Simon said.

"The child is a boy," Magdalena said.

Simon nodded.

"Look around you, Simon Morgenwraithe. We are all orphans," Magdalena said. "You, me, the Blankenship boy, and Helena. If we do nothing, the queen will also become an orphan—just before they kill her."

Magdalena bent over and transformed into a wolf. And she was gone.

Helena and Simon finished preparing new beds.

Helena yawned.

"And I thought we had much to think about, before."

"Aye," Simon said. "I hope that we are able to rest after such a visit."

Simon's stomach growled.

Helena scowled.

"I heard that! I am also hungry. If I wake to the smell of roasted meat, I may kiss that boy."

"I might, as well," Simon said. They laughed and lay down. They were asleep immediately.

Simon was startled awake.

Boone announced his arrival with a whispered yell.

"I'm back! Don't roast me!"

Simon stretched.

"Try not to wake Helena. She needs sleep more than food at this moment."

"Very well," Boone said. "I have a deer and two boars to dress. And I bagged something I haven't been able to bring down for a long time. I thought you might want to give it a try, so I left it alive."

"What's that?" Simon asked.

Boone grinned.

"A wolf."

FORTY-FIVE

Boone looked over his shoulder as he ran down the hill. Simon raced behind him, crashing through the trees, with Helena on his heels.

Boone stumbled and Simon almost ran him over.

Boone waved his hand. He was out of breath. Simon ran on ahead.

He stopped in a small clearing.

"No...," he whispered.

The Lady Magdalena lay on the ground with an arrow through her upper leg. She writhed and moaned. She changed part of the way into a wolf and then back into a woman.

"Oh, no," Boone said. "I didn't...why is she...? What are we going to do, Simon? She was running straight at me!"

"It is a sign, from the gods!" Helena said. "Cut her throat and be done with it!"

"Maybe she's right," Boone said.

"And maybe I don't want to remain a dragon

forever!"

"She's not going to lift the curse, Simon!" Boone cried. "I'd wager she doesn't even know how!"

"I would wager the same!" Helena said. "She stood right in front of you and refused to lift the curse, knowing you could send her to hell with one breath! She's bloody mad, I tell you!"

"It does not end this way," Simon said.

"Let's discuss this for a moment—" Boone said.

"I am the rightful King of the Kingdom of Morgenwraithe!" Simon roared. "The very day I sit my backside on that chair, I will be expected to speak sound judgment! And my judgment says the sorceress does not die this day—and she does not die by my hand!"

Boone cleared his throat.

"Very well. Then, what do we do with her? She's the one with the magic, and she's not long for this world without it. If she was gut-shot, she would be dead already. But the way she's bleeding, it won't matter for long."

"It would be good to know if her house remains under guard," Simon said.

"Aye," Boone said. "That would be good to—wait just a hairy minute! Do you mean to take her to her own house—in the middle of the day? Do you hear the words coming from your own lips?"

"I doubt they're guarding her house anymore," Helena said. "You killed a good one-hundred and thirty-three of their men."

Boone's face filled with a morbid disgust.

"Were you bloody counting them? Men on fire, screaming, and you were counting them?"

Helena crossed her arms.

"I meant nothing by it. I…I like numbers."

"You were all for putting the witch out of her misery a few minutes ago, and now you're on his side!" Boone said.

"I'm on my own side, Boone Blankenship, and I will thank you kindly to stop acting like my mother!"

"Don't you mean acting like your father?"

"I meant what I said!"

"STOP IT THIS INSTANT!" Simon roared.

"I will fly as low as I can, and land outside of the village," Simon said. "Boone, you will have to find a horse, and take Magdalena to her house. We can only pray that she can stay alive and awake long enough to tell you what to do."

Boone shook his head.

"You want me to steal a horse—in broad bloody daylight—to save the woman who cursed you? This just gets better all the time. Can you imagine—if I'm caught stealing a horse and they run me through for it? Or take off my head? The gods will have a laugh at that one, they will."

"You only need to 'borrow' a horse," Simon said. "We'll take it back."

"Aye, we may as well return all your books, while

we're at it. You know, as long as we're settling up."

"I'm going, too," Helena said.

"Like hell, you are," Boone said.

"Like hell, I am!"

"Simon...,"

"She's going with you," Simon said. "You may need all of us, Boone."

"Don't tell me you're—?"

Simon pointed a talon into the air.

"Full moon tonight. Did you forget?"

Boone let his head fall back. He squeezed his eyes shut.

"Yes, I did. You're not—you're not still planning to go to the castle! Not after all of this!"

"I will have time to help you."

"You will not!" Boone said. "If you transform anywhere near the village, you will be caught—and so will we!"

"You make those terrible, terrible sounds each time?" Helena asked.

Simon looked at Boone before he answered.

"It...hurts."

"Hurts," Boone muttered. "It is like every soul in hell is crying out in agony."

"I will make my distance on the opposite side of the village, and I will hurry," Simon said.

Magdalena rolled over and cried out in pain.

Boone bent over her.

"Can you hear me, my...Lady?"
Boone glanced angrily at Simon. He jumped.
Magdalena took hold of his hand.
"Yes," she whispered.

"We will take you to your home—on the back of
the dragon," Boone said. He watched eagerly for her
reaction. She closed her eyes and nodded.

Boone and Helena lifted Magdalena onto Simon's
back. They were careful, but could not avoid putting
pressure on the arrow shaft. Magdalena screamed and
fell unconscious.

The takeoff was difficult. It took much of their
energy to hold themselves and the unconscious woman
on the dragon's back. They had cuts on their arms and
legs. The dragon's back was made for its defense—not
for carrying passengers.

When it was no longer necessary for Simon to flap
his wings at full strength, the ride became smoother.
Boone and Helena relaxed and tried to let their tired
limbs rest. But then Magdalena began to regain
consciousness. She moaned. She began to turn into the
wolf again.

"No! No!" Boone shouted. Simon heard him, but
there was nothing he could do.

Magdalena's transformations faded in and out—
never quite becoming wolf or woman.

Boone patted her face.

"Wake up! You're going to kill us all!"

And then the rains came.

Simon landed. Boone helped Helena down. She fell to her knees and tried to get up to help with Magdalena. But she slipped twice in the mud and gave up.

Boone got Magdalena down and pulled her beneath the trees. Simon held his outstretched wings over them. Twenty minutes later, the rain slackened and stopped.

Boone stood. He shook the rain from his hair and wiped his face. Thunder continued to roll.

"The rain will be back. Slow walking, for man or horse. I'd better be moving."

"Fewer people about," Simon said. "And fewer in the streets."

"And fewer willin' to stalk down the dragon-man whose screams are lighting up the night," Boone said.

"Yes, that's what I'm hoping," Simon said.

"And the minstrels will sing, 'Good King Simon had an optimistic mind. 'Til the day they chopped off his head and shoved it up his behind!'"

Simon turned aside quickly and a small tree burst into flame.

Helena jumped backward.

"I never! I cannot believe I have thrown in my lot with the likes of you!"

Boone set off through the woods. He pointed his thumb over his shoulder.

"I'm off to find a horse," he said to Simon. "She's

all yours."

FORTY-SIX

Jaclyn climbed out of bed early, feeling happier than she had in years. She stretched her arms and yawned. She hummed. And then she stopped.

It will not serve me well to display such a quick change of mood. I must make any change gradually, and —

Jaclyn leaped for the chamber pot and vomited.

Three retches later, a girl appeared in the doorway. She was pretty, but not as lovely as Helena. Jaclyn could smell the air of fear and deceit on her. She was definitely under the thumb of Lord Sterling.

"Shall I draw your bath, My Queen?"

Jaclyn wiped her mouth with the back of her hand.

"Yes. I believe that would be a good way to begin this day. Is my mother — ?"

"She is still sleeping, my Queen."

The new handmaid turned to go.

"Oh, yes. Word has come that we expect your father to arrive near midday."

Jaclyn's heart leaped in her chest. She controlled her reaction, knowing the girl would report to the King's Regent.

"Very well," Jaclyn said with a smile. The handmaid left to draw her bath. Jaclyn vomited again.

Jaclyn sat down in her chair and put her hand on her belly.

"I do wish that you would quit what you're doing down there. It will be difficult for me to keep us safe while clutching a chamber pot."

Jaclyn gripped the sides of the bath. Her new handmaid was stronger than Helena, and far less gentle. She scrubbed Jaclyn's head with a stiff brush. It was all that Jaclyn could do to keep from crying out.

"What is your name?" Jaclyn asked.

"I am called 'Tilda', myqueen."

"You are quite young. Did you have former duties?"

"Yes, my queen," Tilda said proudly. "I worked the Royal stables. It was my duty to groom the steeds for Lord Sterling and his officers."

Tilda's pride was reflected in her washing of Jaclyn's hair. Jaclyn's head jerked backward, and she was not able to remain silent.

"I'm sorry if I hurt you, my queen," Tilda said. She exhaled heavily.

"We need to change out the water. It pains me to say it, my Queen, but whoever has been washing your hair has not—"

"Listen to me, Stable Girl," Jaclyn snapped. "You

are never again to speak ill of—"

Jaclyn caught herself. She had made a mistake, and she knew it.

Have I been baited by this….this…horse-washer? Did she speak the words fed to her by Lord Sterling?

She would never know. But she knew this exchange would be repeated for Sterling to hear.

"I am sorry, Tilda," Jaclyn said softly. "It was such a shock—to find that someone who was at my side every day could side with that beast. A beast whose idea of gratitude was to roast her alive."

"You needn't apologize to me, my queen," Tilda said. "I spoke out of line. I beg your forgiveness."

Jaclyn patted Tilda's hand. Tilda jerked her hand away in panic.

"You do not need my forgiveness," Jaclyn said. "But you have it, if it makes you feel better."

"May I be excused, my queen?" Tilda said. "I am…I am suddenly feeling ill."

"Yes, of course," Jaclyn said. "Could you hand me my—?"

But Tilda had already run from the room.

She may be strong as an ox, but she is frightened out of her mind, Jaclyn thought.

As well she should be.

Jaclyn dressed and went to the room where her mother was staying. Lady Robinette Lamont stared out of her balcony window as she brushed her hair.

"Did you sleep well, Mother?" Jaclyn asked.

"The only reason I am able to sleep at all in this place is because you are here. I have not slept apart from your father for this many days since we were married!"

Jaclyn took the brush away from her mother and began brushing her hair. Lady Lamont tried to take the brush back.

"By the gods, Jaclyn!" Lady Lamont whispered. "You are the queen! Such things are just not done! There are more servants about than one can count!"

Jaclyn leaned over and whispered into her mother's ear.

"Yes, and they are all spies."

Lady Lamont's eyes grew large. She looked around the room.

"And besides, Mother," Jaclyn said. "Brushing your hair gives me great pleasure. Who would deny the queen anything that brings her pleasure?"

"You seem to be in much better spirits—"

Jaclyn gripped her mother's shoulder. She put a finger to her lips and shook her head slightly. Lady Lamont nodded. She sat back and enjoyed the brushing.

"Father will be here soon," Jaclyn said. "Did someone tell you?"

"Yes. It is to be a good day."

Jaclyn allowed herself a smile.

"Yes. It will."

Lord Lamont arrived as the tables were being prepared for the midday meal. Jaclyn ran to her father and threw her arms around him.

She closed her eyes and smiled. When she opened them, she was looking over her father's shoulder, and into the sneering face of Lord Sterling. Her stomach roiled.

No, she thought. Stop it! Stop it, now!

Jaclyn willed the baby not to cause her to vomit again.

Not in front of Lord Sterling.

Never!

"We have had a feast prepared in your honor, Lord Lamont!" Sterling raised his ever-present cup.

"The first gathering of the Queen, the King that grows within her and both proud grandparents!"

"Now, Lord Sterling," Lady Lamont said. "Let us not forget that the child could be boy or girl!"

Sterling took a drink and wiped his mouth. He had gotten an early start on the day.

"Balderdash!" Sterling sang out. "Let us not bring such negativity to bear on such a glorious day — shall we, My Lady?"

Lady Lamont wore a worried expression.

"Boys!" Sterling yelled. Two of his tasters ran into the dining hall.

"Two new wine-skins! At once! No, make that three! Lord Lamont and I have much to celebrate!"

Jaclyn looked at her father's face. She knew his

position in the Kingdom would have him drinking into the night with Sterling, Raynard, and the other officers.

Lucien walked into the dining hall, wearing his battle gear. He and three young members of his guard were laughing at something one of them said. They stopped and fell silent when they saw that they were being stared at.

Sterling was not only staring, he was incensed.

The King and his friends were sweating and covered in mud. A team of servants scurried behind them to clean the floor.

"Lord Lamont," Lucien said. "It is good to see you."

Lamont bowed.

"It is my honor to be welcomed into your home, Your Grace."

"I will clean up and join you—" Lucien began.

"We shall be here the rest of the day, my king," Sterling said with a wave of his hand. "There is no need to hurry. It could take hours to clear away the mud and sweat!"

Sterling laughed. No one else dared.

Raynard, Captain of the Guard, stepped to Sterling's side.

"Begging your pardon, Lord Sterling. Tonight is the full moon—"

Jaclyn shuddered. She had forgotten that fact.

Sterling had not.

"The dragon would not dare show himself so soon

after his unfortunate…"

Sterling's eyes flicked toward Jaclyn.

"Escape."

"We cannot read the dragon's mind, Lord—" Lucien began.

Sterling waved his arms.

"It has rained for three days with no sign of stopping!" Sterling yelled. "Miserable weather—for man or beast! He will be cowered in a cave somewhere, licking his wounds—probably somewhere far away, and safe! Near the sea, perhaps!"

Lucien scowled in embarrassment. His friends took their leave quickly.

Sterling interrupted the meal with various toasts. Each of them began with increasingly drunken and clumsy efforts to get to his feet. Most of the toasts referred to the certainty that the Royal Child was, without a doubt, the heir to the throne of Morgenwraithe.

Jaclyn gave silent thanks to Magdalena's revelation that the child was indeed a boy. If not for that knowledge, Sterling's words would have frightened her.

What would Sterling do if she gave birth to a girl?

She did not want to entertain such thoughts.

At long last, Sterling excused himself to go to the privy.

Lord Lamont stood while Sterling exited. He remained standing. Lamont stepped to Jaclyn's side and offered her his hand. She took it and stood. He hugged her. While they stood he moved slightly, moving between Jaclyn and the others at the table. He took her hand in both of his and leaned his mouth to her ear.

"Guard this with your life."

Lamont pressed the piece of parchment into Jaclyn's hand.

Jaclyn could barely hide her excitement.

What was this note that her father had taken great care to pass to her? Was it good news? Or bad?

She could not read her father's face. Her mother did not seem to know anything had passed between them.

The meal came to an end, at last. Everyone was excused, except for Sterling, Raynard, and Lord Lamont. Lamont held his cup aloft at Jaclyn. He smiled, showing his reluctance to spend the rest of the day and night drinking with Sterling and his men. But he was an officer of the Kingdom, and drink with them, he must.

Jaclyn's hands trembled as she reached the door to her private quarters. Tilda waited outside.

"Will you be needing anything—?" Tilda asked."

"No," Jaclyn said sharply. "I believe I will have a little nap."

She hurried inside and opened the note.

She could not believe it.

Simon. The man, Simon. In the dungeon. At midnight.

Her heart raced.

And she was sick again.

FORTY-SEVEN

Boone was back in less than two hours. The rains came again. The horse was frightened. Simon stepped back into the trees.

Magdalena was conscious, but weak. The bleeding had slowed.

"That wasn't so bad," Boone said. "I saw no one at the stables. The stable boy was probably asleep in the loft. That's where I would be on a day like this."

"You would probably have some innocent milkmaid cornered in the hay," Helena said.

"That's an even better idea," Boone said. "Pleasure, and then sleep."

Boone stepped next to Simon.

"Do you have clothes?"

"Yes."

"How many more do you have?" Boone asked.

"These are the last of them."

"Well, we'll have to look under the witch's mattress again, won't we?"

Magdalena winced. Boone and Helena helped Magdalena onto the horse's back. Boone tried to help Helena on, but Magdalena was too weak to hold herself.

Helena felt something against her foot. She looked down. Simon slipped his tail out of the trees. Helena stepped on it and mounted the horse behind Boone.

"Please, try to stay a woman until we get you home," Boone said to Magdalena.

He shook his head.

"I sound like a madman."

Simon circled low over the trees. He flew well away from the village, making his way to the side of town opposite Magdalena's house. His course took him within sight of Islemar.

Would that I had time to make my transformation in the safety of Islemar, he thought.

He had never been discovered while transforming near the sea. The crashing waves and the high seawalls covered and dispersed all sounds—even the horrific ones he made.

But he would not have time. He had only the hours of darkness to help Magdalena, and to carry his message to Jaclyn.

In his solitude, Simon's conscious spoke to him.

You heard it yourself, only hours ago. Magdalena has already spoken to Jaclyn. She gave her a message of hope. She let her know she was not alone, and that she should not despair. It was truly possible that the

Kingdom could be rescued from its horrible state.

Magdalena told Jaclyn, in so many words, that her handmaid—no, her friend—was alive.

And that could only mean one thing. Helena was with him. She was alive, and she was a friend of the dragon.

Her friends were together. And trying to…what? Could Jaclyn believe that Magdalena and Simon might be conspiring….together?

Simon shook his head. For a moment, he had been in such deep thought he did not know where he was. He regained his bearings and flew down into a valley. The valley's walls did not perform as well as those surrounding Islemar, but they would have to do.

With perhaps a half hour left until the moon reached the horizon, Simon laid on the ground. He was already tired. And what a night he had in store—the gut-wrenching transformation, followed by a run of several miles to reach Magdalena's house. And these events would occur while everyone in the realm knew he was in his human body until the next moon.

His transformation took place in the middle of a thunderstorm. That much was fortunate.

Simon made it to Magdalena's house without seeing a single person. He heard baying dogs in the distance, but he did not know if they came from a hunting party or not. He fell against the frame of

Magdalena's door—wet, and exhausted. He knocked.

Helena answered the door.

Boone was asleep in a chair. Magdalena lay on the same table where Boone was rescued. Simon held his breath until he saw Magdalena's chest rise and fall.

Helena held up the arrowhead and shaft between her fingers.

"I want to be a sorceress," she said. "That was incredible!"

"Well, I was thinking about making you First Knight, but—"

"I can do both," Helena said. "Who says I can't do both?"

"If anyone could do it, My Lady, it would be you. Has she been awake?"

"She was awake most of the time," Helena said. "I made the potion. Boone said the words. He's good with words—not so good with things like crow's eyes and spiders."

Boone stirred.

"People should not find comfort in the presence of spiders and bird's eyes," he said.

"You cut the skins off of animals, but you're afraid of spiders!"

"Everyone has to eat," Boone said. "I am not afraid of meat. If you want to eat spiders, then go right ahead. You may have my share."

Boone crossed the floor and peeked out of the

door.

"Did anyone see you?" he asked.

"I don't think so," Simon said. "The storm came at just the right time. I believe it covered my...noises."

Simon pointed at Magdalena.

"How long has the arrow been out?"

"Most of an hour," Boone said. "We will wait until she wakes up and treat the wound with the rest of the potion. We'll put her in her bed and leave."

Boone looked Simon in the eye.

"Can I talk you out of this? From what Helena has told me, Magdalena has already led the queen to believe Helena is alive."

Simon bit his lip.

"I just..."

Boone stepped close to Simon's ear, where Helena could not hear.

"I know why. Please, be careful."

FORTY-EIGHT

Jaclyn hummed while she braided her mother's hair.

Lady Lamont turned to look at her daughter.

"Jaclyn, there are scores of maidens who would consider it an honor to braid the hair of the Queen's mother! What has gotten in to you, child? Not that I am complaining, mind you. It does my heart good to see you happy, at last. You have had us worried…"

Jaclyn placed her hand on her tummy.

"The little Prince takes great pleasure in disrupting my insides, I'm afraid. But he seems to have made his peace with me in the last two days."

Jaclyn returned her hands to her mother's hair.

She swore.

"Jaclyn!" Lady Lamont scolded. And then she laughed.

"That is no language for a Queen!"

"I am expected to rule a people, yet braiding hair gets the best of me!" Jaclyn said.

Lady Lamont stood.

"Let's have a maid or two come and help you—"
"No," Jaclyn snapped.
"What is the matter?" Lady Lamont whispered.

Jaclyn whispered into her mother's ear.
"Trust no one, Mother. Especially here."
Lady Lamont sank into her chair, and Jaclyn
started over.

At dusk, there was a knock at the door.
"Enter," Jaclyn said.
Lucien stepped into the room. He bowed his head.
"My queen. Good evening, Lady Lamont."
Lady Lamont stood.
"Good evening, Your Grace."

Lucien was sweating and covered in mud. He was
still in his battle gear, the same as he had worn into the
dining hall. His face also displayed the foul depression
that resulted from Lord Sterling's dressing down.
Jaclyn felt a twinge of pity for Lucien. She stepped
across the floor and kissed his dirty cheek.
Lucien stammered and blushed.
"I...it has been a long day. I wish you a good
night, Lady Lamont."
"Thank you, Your Grace," Lady Lamont said.

Lucien left the room.
Lady Lamont smiled at her daughter.
"I'll bet he is not all that tired. You may finish my
hair in the morning if you like."

"Mother, please!" Jaclyn said. "While you and father are here? By the gods!"

Jaclyn saw movement outside the window. She walked over and looked out. A lone eagle soared high across the sky.

Jaclyn's stomach rumbled. She put her hand there again as she watched the great bird fly.

We will meet the true King this night, Little One. It will be our secret.

An hour later, Jaclyn crept to the King's bed chamber. She pushed open the door. Lucien's dirty clothes and boots lay in a heap on the floor. Jaclyn wrinkled her nose. Lucien lay snoring, sprawled across the entire bed, leaving mud smeared along the linens.

Jaclyn tip-toed into the room. Lucien's dagger sheath lay open on top of his shed trousers. Jaclyn took it. She stepped toward the corridor and then froze.

Voices.

Her heart raced as she waited for them to pass.

One of the voices belonged to Sterling. She was certain of it.

Jaclyn peered out into the corridor. She walked in the opposite direction opposite of fading voices. She stepped outside into the courtyard.

"Who goes there?"

Jaclyn shuddered.

King's Guard. They are everywhere.

That night, in the courtyard, there were two of

them.

"It is the Queen!" Jaclyn said. "Try your best not to kill me, if you please."

The men bowed their heads.

"Forgive us, my Queen. We were not expecting you. And we must be on high alert. It is the night of the full—"

"The full moon," Jaclyn said dismissively, with a wave of her hand. "Yes, we must remain ever vigilant in defense against the scary old dragon!"

"It is our sworn duty, my Queen."

"Has it occurred to you, that it is most unlikely that the dragon will use the doors?"

"This is our assigned post—"

"I see. Yet, I have just come from the King's chambers, where the King sleeps, soundly. There are three windows there, and yet I saw no guards outside of them. Nor in the corridor outside."

The guards looked at each other helplessly.

"We beg you to return inside, my Queen."

Jaclyn sighed.

"I could not sleep. The air has become so stuffy in this old place. I intend to take a walk about the garden."

"Please, My Queen, it is not safe—"

"You dare to argue against my wishes?" Jaclyn snapped. "Maybe I should bring this matter to the attention of Lord Sterling—"

"No. I mean, I beg your forgiveness, My Queen.

We will move nearer to the King's quarters. Your insight is correct."

Jaclyn nodded and strolled away. When the guards were gone, she hurried along the shadows and toward the entrance to the dungeon.

The dungeon was unoccupied and had no guard assigned to it. There was no light inside of the guard quarters.

Jaclyn turned a corner in the corridor and heard a sound behind her. She took out the King's dagger and walked back in the direction she had come. She waited at the corner.

When she saw an arm reaching in the dark, she grabbed it and pulled.

The boy lost his footing and fell to the floor. Jaclyn fell upon him and held the dagger to his throat.

"Who are you?" Jaclyn demanded in a whisper. "And why are you following me? I could have your head for this!"

"I mean no harm, my Queen!" the boy cried. "On the contrary! I am on your side!"

Jaclyn shook the dagger angrily.

"What do you mean, on my side?"

The boy turned his head toward the dungeon door.

"I was there, that day, my Queen. The day the dragon was set free."

"You are lying!" Jaclyn sneered.

"No, my Queen," the boy shook his head. His eyes were large and full of torment.

"I am the lowest in the King's army. I run errands for the officers. I had only just received a sword—

"Lord Sterling took it from me. He…he used it to…he used it on…your handmaiden."

Jaclyn lowered the dagger. She covered her mouth with her hand.

"I am so sorry, my queen," the boy continued, as tears stained his cheeks.

"I cannot rest. I cannot sleep. It is but a matter of time before they determine that I am no good for anything. And then they will kill me."

"Go back to your quarters," Jaclyn said. "The passage of time will mend your wounds. You must—"

The boy climbed to his feet.

"You hate them," he said.

"What?" Jaclyn said. She could not believe what she was hearing.

"Lord Sterling. Raynard. Perhaps, even King Lucien," the boy said. "I can see it in your eyes."

"If you have the wish to die, you are going about it properly. Such talk is—"

"Such talk is the truth," the boy said. "If I can see it, then so will others."

"What do you want from me?" Jaclyn cried in a whispered scream.

"I hear things—whispers."

"You must go now," Jaclyn said.

"Please, my queen. Tell me—"

"If you wish to live to see the sunrise, you must go now," Jaclyn said. She turned away.

"The dragon. The true King. Do you know him?"

Jaclyn spun around holding the dagger.

She was beyond angry. But in the boy's eyes she saw only desperate hope. The boy did not move when Jaclyn stepped directly in front of him.

"What is your name?" she asked.

"Oliver, my queen."

She leaned toward his ear.

"If you are able to remain silent, and to remain alive.

"Yes, I know the true king."

The boy burst into tears. He fell to his knees. Jaclyn put her hand on his shoulder.

The boy tenderly took Jaclyn's hand in both of his and kissed it.

"You are true, and just! I will follow you to the ends of the world, my queen!"

Jaclyn pulled the boy to his feet.

"I prefer followers who continue to breathe," Jaclyn said. "Go!"

The boy ran away.

FORTY-NINE

Simon stood in the shadows, looking up at the massive stone wall of his family's home.

Castle Morgenwraithe.

By his birthright, he should be asleep at this moment in the magnificent four-post bed inside the King's chambers. The bed had taken multiple craftsmen most of a year to build.

He should be asleep, lying next to his beautiful Queen, who would be…..

Who would have been my Queen? He thought.

Would my father have made the same arrangement—if he had lived?

Simon shuddered. Chills flooded him.

It was most likely. Jaclyn Lamont and he were the same age. Lord Nicolas Lamont had been the Kingdom's Viceroy since well before…

Before the world went to hell.

These thoughts did not comfort Simon. He held onto the trunk of a tree as he looked up. His hands trembled.

This is the most foolish thing I have ever done, he thought. In a life full of foolish behaviors.

In human form, he would fall to one arrow. Or one blow or stab from a sword.

But there was one more thing he could not bear.

He could not bear to go one more day without seeing Queen Jaclyn Lamont Morgenwraithe—

Face-to face.

There was no turning back. Lord Lamont had agreed to pass Jaclyn a note at his request. She would wait for him in the dungeon at midnight.

Or she would not.

If she was not there, he did not know if his heart could take the pain.

But he placed every ounce of his hope on her being there to meet him.

Simon ran the distance between the guard towers. He caught his breath, standing against the wall. The secondary castle gate was nearest the entrance to the dungeon. He crept in that direction, hiding in the shadows. The gate was chained, but he was able to squeeze through. If there were guards stationed there, they were not on high alert. Asleep, perhaps.

Simon ran between patches of darkness, toward the dungeon entrance he had last seen during his escape, as the feared dragon. He dove through the outer door and stopped to catch his breath.

It was the night of the full moon. And yet, the

army of Morgenwraithe did not fear him.

For this, Simon was glad.

And he was determined to make them pay for ignoring the fire that burned within his heart whether he was man or beast.

Simon crept down the corridor, staying in the shadows provided by flickering torches. Only a few of them were lit. He breathed a sigh of relief when he saw that the guard room was dark.

He stepped through the dungeon door. He looked up at the shackles and chains that had almost spelled his end.

His foot kicked a stone across the floor.

"Hello?" he heard a voice.

Her voice.

Simon swallowed.

At long last...

"Who goes there?" the voice of two members of the King's Guard echoed loudly off of the stone.

It was the same two that Jaclyn met outside in the courtyard.

A cold, strong hand grabbed her wrist.

"You!"

An angry face pulled Jaclyn close.

"Lord Sterling was right!" the guard sneered. "She is up to something! There is someone else here!"

Jaclyn squealed. She jerked her arm free and ran toward the door.

She could not tell what was happening. The two guards had the intruder surrounded.

He was unarmed. And helpless.

"You have dared to invade the home of King Lucien, King of the Realm!" a guard shouted. "Show yourself, or you die this night!"

"I do not recognize your King!" came a shout in the darkness.

"Then you shall die at the hand of his Guard!" came the reply.

"No!" Queen Jaclyn shouted.

One guard crumpled to the floor. Lord Nicolas Lamont pulled on the hilt of his sword, which was buried in the back of the dead guard.

The second guard jumped in front of Lamont, his sword held high.

"Traitorous bastard!" the guard growled. Lamont could do nothing but raise his arm in defense.

The guard brought down his sword.

But he stopped. His eyes bulged, and he crumpled to the floor, face-first.

A dagger was buried to the hilt between his shoulder blades.

Torchlight reflected on the handle of the dagger. Jaclyn knew the dagger at once.

It was hers.

Jaclyn squinted into the shadows.

Simon had saved her father. She just knew it.

The heaving profile of Lord Nicolas Lamont

hovered over the two fallen guards.

"Father!" Jaclyn cried. She ran to him. Lord Lamont pushed her aside. He ran to the middle of the dungeon floor.

Jaclyn squinted and peered into the darkness.

"Simon?" she called. "Are you there?"

There was no answer.

Lord Lamont knelt and pulled with all his strength at the heavy iron grate in the floor.

"What is this, Father?" Jaclyn asked.

"The pit of Morgenwraithe," Lamont said. "Also known as the 'Portal to Hell'. You must help me."

The pit cover was far from the only two lit torches inside the dungeon entrance. It was pitch dark in the middle of the room.

Nicolas grabbed Jaclyn's arm.

"Do not let go of me, Jaclyn," he said. "To fall into this abyss is certain death. But we cannot allow these guards to be discovered."

They pulled on the heavy iron grate with all their might. It would not budge.

"Jaclyn."

Jaclyn froze.

"Do not be afraid," Simon whispered. "I will help you."

Jaclyn felt another hand grip her arm, alongside her father's. Chills flooded her body. She strained her eyes, but it was no use. She could not see his face.

The grate gave way, a little at a time. They pulled until the grate had moved a little more than a foot.

Lord Lamont pushed the two fallen guards through the opening. Lamont, Jaclyn, and Simon strained and pulled the grate back into place. Simon let go of Jaclyn's arm.

"No!" Jaclyn screamed. She reached out and grabbed Simon's hand, in the darkness.

"You must take this!"

She pressed Helena's locket into his hand.

"We have to get out of here, now!" Lord Lamont said.

"Simon!" Jaclyn cried. "Where are you?"

"Here!" Simon said. He stood in the doorway of the dungeon exit. Jaclyn could see only his silhouette in the dim light.

She ran in that direction.

They heard the shouts of men approaching through the main entrance corridor.

"No!" Lord Lamont growled. He grabbed Jaclyn's arm.

"We have to go, Jaclyn!"

Simon heard the voices as well. He turned to run. His foot kicked against something in the floor. He heard the sound of steel sliding across the stone floor. The dim light reflected momentarily off of the blade of a short sword. Simon picked it up without stopping.

"I will leave something for you, in our special place!" he whispered into the darkness.

"Do not leave me!" Jaclyn cried.

Simon's silhouetted disappeared through the double-door corridor.

Lord Lamont dragged Jaclyn by the hand through the same exit.

Lord Lamont passed by the main entrance when the first person reached the door. It was King Lucien, clad only in his muddy battle trousers.

Lamont did not know what to do. He could not get Jaclyn through the other door without being seen.

Lucien crumpled to the floor. Standing over the king, was a boy holding an iron soup pot. The boy looked at Lamont briefly, his eyes wide open with fear.

"Thank you," Jaclyn whispered. "Now, run, you foolish boy!"

The boy ran. Father and daughter were right on his heels.

Lamont and Jaclyn disappeared into the night. They sneaked into the castle, and to the guest quarters. They climbed into bed.

"What is happening, Nicolas?" Lady Robinette Lamont whispered to her husband.

Lamont patted his wife's cheek.

"Shh," he whispered.

"Jaclyn and I have been here all night. Remember that."

Lady Lamont rolled over. She saw Jaclyn lying on

the bed opposite her. They stared at each other, their eyes wide with fear.

And none of them slept.

FIFTY

Jaclyn bolted upright in her bed. Lord and Lady Lamont did the same.

Someone was rapping loudly upon their door. It was not yet dawn.

"Come in!" Jaclyn called.

Her new handmaid, Tilda, opened the door quickly. She lowered her eyes and dipped her knees.

"Begging your pardon, My Queen. Lord and Lady Lamont. It is just…it is just that—"

A sudden commotion sounded in the corridor.

"We have found him! He is here!"

Jaclyn swung her legs out of the bed and onto the floor.

"Please, my Queen," Tilda said. "Let me fetch your robe!"

"What is going on?" Jaclyn insisted. "Who has been found?"

"The king…he was not in his chambers. There was quite the panic—"

"Lucien—?" Jaclyn pushed past Tilda and into the corridor.

Tilda ran after Jaclyn and wrapped her robe around her shoulders.

Jaclyn heard Lucien's voice as he climbed the stairs.

Lord Sterling and Raynard were at his heels.

Lucien reached the top of the stairs. He swayed on his feet and grabbed the back of his head.

"What were you doing in the dungeon—in the middle of the night?" Sterling sneered. "There are very few lit torches—even along the corridor. It is small wonder you fell and hit your head—you could have killed yourself! What kind of legacy would that leave, Your Gr—?"

Lucien spun on his heels. His fists were clenched, a fact noted by both Sterling and Raynard.

"I told you, Uncle!" Lucien growled. "I did not fall! I was struck—from behind!"

Sterling and Raynard exchanged a look, and slight smiles.

"Then we most definitely have a problem!" Sterling said. "There is one among us who has risked certain death, in order to give the King a massive headache!"

"It was him!" Lucien snarled.

"It was who?" Sterling asked, nonchalantly.

"The dragon! My brother!" Lucien cried out. "He

was here! I know it!"

Sterling scowled. He grabbed Lucien by his bare shoulder and pushed him through the door and into the King's chambers. He looked down the corridor and met Jaclyn's eyes.

Jaclyn saw distrust. And hate. She ran past Sterling and Raynard and into the King's chambers.

To comfort her husband.

Sterling leaned close to Raynard's ear.

"Get some men down there. Light the place and search it."

"Surely, you do not believe—" Raynard said.

"No!" Sterling replied through clenched teeth. "I do not believe the dragon-boy was within miles of here. If I did, I would have taken precautions, wouldn't I?"

"Yes, My Lord," Raynard said.

Sterling sniffed the air. He narrowed his eyes.

"There is something…." he hissed. "There is something amiss—something I cannot put my finger on."

"I will send my men," Raynard said. He turned to go.

"Wait," Sterling said.

"Did we have guards at the home of the Sorceress?"

Raynard shook his head.

"No, my Lord. You said—"

"I know very well what I said!" Sterling snapped. "Send two guards there immediately. And do not send boys."

MY NAME IS SIMON 312

"I'm still replacing the good men who fell to the dragon," Raynard said. "No one volunteers after so many died by dragon fire. And inside the castle at that! We must replenish our numbers from somewhere."

FIFTY-ONE

Simon sneaked along the tree-line, behind Magdalena's house. He froze when he heard rustling in the fallen leaves.

He relaxed when he saw Helena's unmistakable hair.

"Pssst!" Simon whispered. "It's me!"

"She will be fine soon," Boone whispered. "The wound still looks bad, but she is not in much pain—"

Simon held up his hand. He heard voices murmuring—still fairly distant.

Simon swore under his breath.

"I knew Sterling would send someone here!"

"What happened at the castle?" Helena asked.

"There is no time," Simon whispered. "Both of you—go! Now!"

"What are you going to do?" Boone asked.

"We cannot let them find her with an arrow wound," Simon said. "Or questions will arise. Sterling is not stupid."

"I will stay with you," Boone said.

"Me too!" Helena said.

"No!" Simon said. "Get to the cave. That is an order."

Boone grabbed Helena's hand and pulled her away.

"Do you have the dagger?" Helena asked.

"No," Simon said. "I had to use it."

"By the gods!" Boone said. He pulled on Helena's hand, and they disappeared into the night.

Simon crept toward the door to Magdalena's house. Two men appeared, in the uniforms of the King's Guard. They were young and did not carry themselves like hardened soldiers.

These "guards" are not long for this world, behaving as they are, Simon thought.

One of them rapped on the door.

"King's Guard, My Lady! On the King's business!"

They waited. One of them tried the door. It was open. They stepped inside.

Simon ran to the wall where he could hear anything the guards said.

"Sorry for the intrusion, My Lady—"

"Something is wrong here—she's not moving. My Lady? Can you hear me?"

Simon heard Magdalena moan.

"Great Vehallion's ghost!" a guard exclaimed. "She's been pierced with an arrow!"

"You—you stay here with her. I'll alert Lord Sterling!"

Simon was in a state of panic. He could not allow the guard to leave. But he had no weapon.

He flexed his hands. When the guard appeared in the doorway, Simon lowered his shoulder and ran at the guard as hard as he could. The guard never saw him coming. He folded in half around Simon and landed next to the steel-clad wall.

Simon grabbed the guard's head. He closed his eyes and ground his teeth.

He bashed the man's head against the steel. The man moaned.

Simon did it again.

He heard swearing above him. He looked up and saw the terrified face of the other young guard. Simon watched as his fright turned to rage. The young man raised his sword above his head and brought it down. Simon rolled out of the way. The guard swung his sword sideways and tore open Simon's shirt. Simon backed against the wall and had no means of escape.

The wolf hit the guard from the side. It bit down on the young man's shoulder, tearing the flesh as it ripped its jaws from side to side.

The man screamed in agony and then began to cry and to beg.

The wolf released the man's shoulder. It stood on top of him and turned its head to look at Simon. Simon sat on the ground, breathing heavily.

The wolf tilted its head and whined.

Simon looked into the pained face of the crying guard. The guard's fate was inevitable; it was almost certain that he would bleed to death before he could be saved.

To leave him alive would be taking a risk.

Simon pushed himself to his feet.

"He has seen your wound. And my face."

The wolf sank its teeth into the man's neck. And it was over.

Simon looked into the sky. Dawn was coming.

"Come with us to—"

But the wolf bounded away and disappeared—in the opposite direction of their cave.

Boone and Helena were sound asleep when Simon reached the cave. The morning was cold. They huddled together for warmth. Or, for other reasons.

Simon did not disturb them. He lay down on his own bed, the bed made for the dragon. He was asleep instantly.

Simon woke to the heavenly smell of roasted meat.

Simon handed Helena her locket. She burst into tears. She caressed the locket for hours and held it against her heart.

The three of them relived the tales of the previous night.

When Simon finished his account of what happened at the castle, they stared into the crackling fire.

Boone stood and rubbed his face. He put his hand on Simon's shoulder.

"I am truly sorry, my friend. But no experience would have been enough, would it?"

Simon shook his head.

He held his hand in front of him and stared at it.

"I touched her arm—with this hand. I felt the warmth of her skin."

Boone patted Simon's shoulder.

"It is a start, My King."

"Yes," Simon said. "It is a start."

Simon stood and looked outside where the shadows grew long.

"We will travel tonight—to the eastern shore of Islemar. I...have something to do there. And we need a quiet place to rest."

"Do you think we will see Magdalena soon?" Boone asked.

"I should not be surprised," Simon said.

Simon began his walk. He walked further away than he had to. The transformation would be one of pleasure, not pain.

But he wanted time alone, to think.

He had not lied to his friends, but he had feelings about last night he could not share. He did not think his friends would understand.

He walked into a deep gulch, between two high walls of sheer stone.

His transformation, back into the dragon, was only moments away.

Simon did not want to experience the sensations that lay ahead. He did not want to sense the unbounded freedom that accompanied his transformation.

He did not want to feel the physical pleasure. He did not want to feel the rush of adrenaline that would launch him into another eternal sky.

The familiar tingle started in the tips of his fingers. He looked down at them.

"No!" he screamed.

His fingers splayed. They grew in length. His nails grew, beginning with his right hand.

"NO!" Simon screamed again.

He turned and swung his hand into the stone wall as hard as he could. The nails shattered. Blood spurted into the air.

Simon laughed like a madman.

The blood stopped. His nails continued to change.

Simon swore at the top of his lungs. He smashed his hand into the stone again. Nothing happened. Both of his hands changed into talons before his eyes.

Simon threw back his head and screamed.

He lowered his head and ran at the stone wall on the other side of the gulch—

An immense wave of adrenalin coursed through him. He left the ground.

Simon the dragon flew, and he cried.

FIFTY-TWO

The servants finished loading the Royal carriage.

Jaclyn leaned toward her father. She stared at Tilda, who was quite excited to be traveling outside of the village for the first time in her life—and as a handmaid to the Queen!

"Does she have to come with us?" Jaclyn asked quietly.

Lord Lamont could not help but laugh.

"It is the most exciting day of her life—as well as being proper protocol for a Queen when she travels. Anything else would raise suspicion."

"She cannot be trusted," Jaclyn said.

"Of course not, my dear."

Lucien approached them.

"I wish you would come with us," Jaclyn lied with a smile.

Lucien smiled.

"It will be good for you to visit Islemar for a few days. You have not yet visited as Queen. The people will be thrilled to see you. And that is good for the Kingdom."

Jaclyn continued to smile. Lord Lamont bowed his head.

"Well said, your Grace. We will give the people of Islemar your words, and your best wishes."

"Please, do so, Lord Lamont."

The Lamonts arrived in Islemar to great fanfare. The people lined the streets. They cheered and threw flowers before the procession of guards, horses, and the Royal carriage.

A huge feast was prepared for the evening meal. Everyone ate heartily, except for Jaclyn. The Queen did not want a heavy meal to make her sleepy.

She had plans for late that night.

Jaclyn retired to her old bedroom. Tilda knocked gently on the door and opened it.

"Will you be needing anything further, My Queen?"

"Yes, as a matter of fact, I will," Jaclyn said. "Come in."

Tilda stood at attention.

"Yes, my Queen?"

Jaclyn pointed to a chair.

"Sit."

Tilda looked confused but she did as she was told.

Jaclyn stood and walked to her wardrobe. She returned with a flask of wine and two cups.

She poured them both full.

She handed one to Tilda. Tilda was terrified.

"I...I beg your pardon, my Queen."

"It is wine, Tilda. You drink it."

"But...but...I..."

"I am no longer a child, Tilda," Jaclyn said. "And neither are you. Drink it."

"But—"

"Your Queen has given you an order."

"Yes, my Queen."

"So, tell me about yourself," Jaclyn said.

"There is not much to tell, My Queen..."

Jaclyn pretended to sip her wine.

"This is excellent wine! Drink up, Tilda!"

"This is...most unusual, My Queen," Tilda stammered.

"Nonsense!" Jaclyn smiled.

"How would you know what is unusual? You have been my handmaid for what—all of a week?"

Tilda stared at her cup.

"I am confused, My Que—"

"Drink," Jaclyn said.

Her smile was gone.

Tilda told story after story about the magnificent steeds she cared for. Jaclyn tried to pay attention. She sipped at her wine while continually filling Tilda's cup.

After two cups of wine, Tilda's stories changed to include tawdry scenes involving stable boys and various members of the King's army. Jaclyn found these stories much more interesting.

When Jaclyn was confident that Tilda would sleep soundly for quite a while, she helped her to her quarters.

Tilda hummed as Jaclyn helped her to bed. She smiled when Jaclyn pulled up the blanket to tuck her in.

"You are so nice!" Tilda said. "You are the best Queen in the world!"

"Sweet dreams, Tilda," Jaclyn whispered.

Jaclyn backed out of the guest room. Tilda's humming grew softer until it turned into snores.

The hour was late and the rest of the castle was silent. Jaclyn took the oil lamp from her room and crept down the corridor toward the servant entrance. She slipped outside and pulled her cloak tightly around her neck. The ever-present winds off of the sea chilled her. She ran across the courtyard and entered the stairwell to the tower.

Jaclyn took the steps two at a time, shrieking and almost falling when she stepped on a mouse.

She reached the top level and its two rooms. She stepped inside the room she had not seen in years—the room that filled her memory and fueled her desires for five long years.

The room still held a bed and a bureau, each covered with heavy, dusty cloth. Jaclyn held the lamp high and searched the dusty floor for signs of footprints. Or…talon prints.

The floor was undisturbed. Jaclyn pulled open the bureau door.

It was empty and contained nothing but an abandoned spider web.

Sadness.

Disappointment.

And fear, gripped Jaclyn's heart.

The possibility had never occurred to her that Simon's words had been empty. That he could make a promise to her and not keep it.

Or worse yet—what if something had happened to him? Something bad. Something terrible. The entire Kingdom wished him dead. What if—?

Jaclyn heard a fluttering sound outside the window.

Her heart raced. He ran to the window and leaned out.

Nothing.

Nothing but the howling wind.

Jaclyn pulled herself up into the window. She crept carefully along its ledge, inching her way out toward the bastion. One more step and she would reach safe footing.

The flurry of bats came out of nowhere. Jaclyn screamed. The bats circled her head, whipping through her hair. She swatted at them with her free hand. Her right foot slipped. She reached for the edge of the bastion and her hand became tangled in her hair. In her panic she made a fist. She opened her eyes and found herself face-to-face with a terrified bat.

Jaclyn and the bat screeched at each other. Jaclyn lost her balance and waved her arms. A piece of stone broke loose beneath her feet. She fell forward and struck her head.

And the world went black.

Jaclyn woke and raised her head. The bats had moved on, and she was alone again with the roaring wind. She lifted her head and looked down. Her hands were bloody. She pushed herself to her knees.

And then she saw it.

Beneath a large, flat stone, she saw the corner of a piece of parchment.

Jaclyn lifted the stone. The wind whipped at the parchment, threatening to carry it out to sea. Jaclyn snatched it just in time. She held it to her chest and pulled herself back along the window ledge. She reached the window and pulled herself up. She lost her grip momentarily and threw her arm across the window sill. She fell headfirst into the room.

Jaclyn breathed deeply. She held the parchment tightly as she limped toward the lamp. A swirling gust of wind whipped around her, threatening to tear the parchment from her fingers.

Jaclyn swore, cursing at the wind and its evil purposes.

She took the lamp and sat down on the floor,

beside the bed and out of the wind currents.

With trembling hands, she held the parchment in front of her eyes.

My earliest memory is of wanting.
I wanted to learn, to read, to explore.
I wanted my mother to hold me, instead of assigning me to nursemaids.
I wanted my father to hold me in his lap. I wanted to hear him laugh,
and hear him remark to anyone who would listen how intelligent and gifted his son was.
And then, everything was taken away.
And I wanted back everything I had lost.
These were all the wants of a selfish child.
My wants became simpler.
I wanted to live another day.
I wanted to eat.
I wanted to survive.
But there have been many days and nights that all I wanted
Was to die.

All this is behind me now.
I have become a man.
I want my birthright restored.
I want to be the King that the people deserve.
But these desires pale in the light of the want that has burned inside of me for five long years.
I want the friend I cannot have.

I want to look each day upon the face that I cannot touch.

I want the love that my heart has been denied.

I want you.

Your friend,

S

Jaclyn bit her lip. She read the note again, through her eyes that swam with tears. And then she read it again. She held the note in her lap and stared at the ceiling.

She looked at the flickering lamp beside her. She held the note in her right hand.

The note was the ultimate danger.

It was treason.

This single piece of parchment could tear apart the entire Kingdom.

It would not merely cost her the crown —

It could cost her life.

Her hand shook as she moved the parchment toward the flame.

She held it there.

One second.

Two.

And then she clutched it to her chest.

"NO!" she screamed into the darkness.

FIFTY-THREE

The dragon circled overhead as twilight fell upon the farm. The youngest girl gathered up her homemade dolls from the front porch. A long shadow passed over her shoulder. She looked up, screamed, and ran inside.

"Father! The dragon has returned!"

The older sister cowered. The two boys ran for their bows.

The farmer sat on a chair in the middle of the one-room house. His tattered boots lay beside him, the holes having grown large enough to make the soles nearly useless. His youngest son had just taken a pot of hot water from the fire to pour into the pan where the man soaked his feet.

"Put down your bows," the man said to his sons.

"But, Father," the oldest boy said. "The beast has taken you once—we may not be so fortunate the next time!"

"How many times have I told you, Luke," the man said. "The tales you hear in the village are based on nothing. Nothing, but the frightened talk of women and cowardly men."

"Father, I do not need the words of others to know the danger of great flying beasts with sharp teeth and breath made of fire!"

The man stood and limped to the door. His sons followed him, carrying their bows. The man placed his hand on the door handle.

"If either of you passes through this door with a bow, I will consider it disrespect."

The boys dropped their bows and followed their father outside.

The dragon circled once more. He circled again.

Something fell from the dragon's talons and plummeted down at them. The children screamed and ran for the door.

A bundle of burlap struck the ground at the man's feet.

"What is it, Father?" the youngest girl asked.

"I'll wager that it is a severed head!" cried the youngest boy.

"Be quiet!" the man said. They looked to the sky. The dragon was gone.

The man stood over the bundle. He untied the rope that bound it.

There were two more bundles inside of the burlap. The man unwrapped the first one. His jaw fell slack. He wrapped his hand around the jeweled hilt and held up the gleaming sword. Its blade reflected the sun in a dazzling display of color.

The man opened the second bundle.

Inside that package were two new shirts, two new pairs of trousers—

And a new pair of boots.

The man held the boots before his face. He breathed in the heavenly scent of newly tanned leather. A tear ran down his cheek.

He picked up the burlap bag and shook it. It was not empty. The man looked inside and found—

Five large pieces of hard-rock candy.

I hope you have enjoyed the first book in the I, Dragon series. If you did, then please consider leaving a review at Amazon. You know what they say—the way to a man's heart is through an Amazon review. It is SO easy to leap-frog into the position of being one of my favorite people. The link for the book is here:

http://amzn.to/2diGY3F

Want to keep reading Simon's story?
Here's the link to Book 2
Rebellion

http://amzn.to/2iBPOij

Please visit
www.nathanroden.com

Sign up for the newsletter to receive future release information, exclusive content, early reader information, and future contests and giveaways.

Also by Nathan Roden

The Wylie Westerhouse Paranormal Fantasy Series

Book 1 Ghosts on Tour
http://amzn.to/1Vhn36c

Book 2 The Dark Stage
http://amzn.to/1Y4NMCc

Book 3 The Lightning's Kiss
http://amzn.to/29XO8xo

Nathan Roden lives in South Central Texas
with his wife and two in-and-out sons, and more
dogs and cats than is necessary.

To grab the free novelette and your two free
short stories, and find out what's coming up, visit

www.nathanroden.com

Connect with Nathan:

BLOG: nathanroden.com

FACEBOOK:www.facebook.com/nathan.rode
n.books

TWITTER: twitter.com/WNathanRoden

GOODREADS:
www.goodreads.com/user/show/41141121-nathan-
roden

PINTEREST:
www.pinterest.com/nathanroden/

73522207R00207

Made in the USA
San Bernardino, CA
06 April 2018